I0817813

# CALICO THUNDER RIDES AGAIN

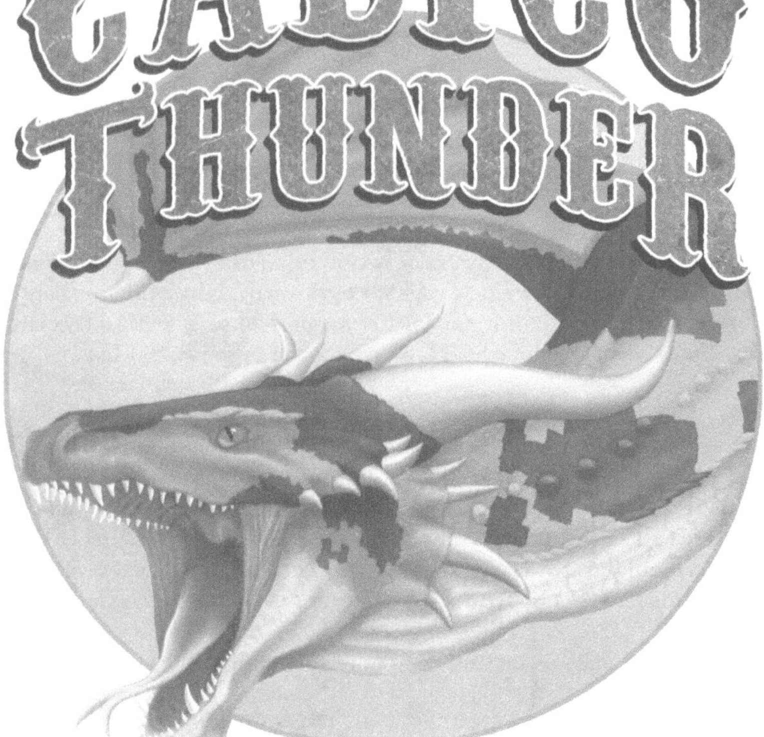

T. A. HERNANDEZ

CALICO THUNDER RIDES AGAIN



Cover art and design by T. A. Hernandez

ISBN-13: 978-1-7340330-0-7
ISBN-10: 1-7340330-0-2

*To Alex—Thank you for always walking by my side through life's many adventures— the happy ones, the hard ones, and everything in between.*

# PROLOGUE

## A NIGHT AT THE CIRCUS

They sat in the front row of the grandstands under the canvas of the big top, just two ordinary spectators in a crowd full of smiling faces. The boy was wide-eyed and silent, but Harvey found himself humming along to a familiar, bouncing tune as the rich tones of the brass band filled the air. A half-eaten bag of roasted peanuts lay on the bench beside him, and occasionally, a whiff of their warm, hearty smell found its way to his nose, evoking memories of his own childhood visits to the circus.

Ah, to be a boy again, if only for a day. Inside the tent, none of his problems mattered, and just being here made him feel decades younger. At his age, despite the circumstances that had brought him here in the first place, that was good enough.

He glanced down at his companion, who reached for a handful of peanuts as he craned his tiny neck to watch the agile trapeze artists soaring overhead. The lithe man hanging upside-down from a swinging bar caught his partner by the arms and held her for the space of a heartbeat before sending her flying again.

The center ring below them suddenly ignited with

dancing purple flames, and the crowd let out a collective gasp. The hanging trapeze artist continued to swing back and forth like a pendulum as the flames reached higher, lapping at his dangling hands.

His female companion timed another swing and leaped from her raised platform. She passed right over the fire once...twice...then launched herself into the air and pirouetted so fast it seemed impossible for her partner to catch her.

Harvey gripped the edge of his seat and leaned forward, certain the poor young woman was about to plummet to a fiery death in the flames below.

At the very last second, the man caught her. As her body swung down through the heart of the fire, the violet flames burst into hundreds of white flower petals that fluttered harmlessly toward the grandstands and drifted down, carrying with them the sweet scent of caramel and vanilla.

The petals disappeared before they hit the ground, but the magical illusion had ignited the crowd. Harvey applauded and whistled with the rest of the onlookers as the trapeze artists finished their act and bid them all farewell with waves and a few blown kisses.

Beside him, the boy shoved another handful of peanuts into his mouth. His wide eyes scanned the canvas sidewalls of the tent, but when he didn't see who he was looking for, he turned his attention back to the center ring for the next act.

Harvey shifted uncomfortably in his seat and loosened the tie around his neck. The boy seemed like such a sweet, endearing child. A shame that, like the circus, it was all just an elaborate act.

The spotlight fell on the announcer in the center ring. His magically-amplified voice boomed through the tent like thunder. "Ladies and gentlemen, boys and girls, for our final performance this evening, Strickland's Circus is proud to present a thrilling spectacle unlike any you've seen before." He paused for a few moments as if to let the audience soak in his words. "Everyone give a warm welcome to the fearless queen of the center ring and her extraordinary winged beasts. I present to you, Grace Hawkins!"

He dragged out the vowels of the name as the crowd broke into applause. A young woman in a short red dress with glittering gold accents entered the ring. Contrary to the popular bobbed style of the times, her long hair flowed free behind her like a dark cape. She flashed a radiant smile at the audience and raised both hands in a wave, then turned around and signaled to the four black-clad men standing just at the edge of the lit area. They stepped forward into the light, and a wave of gasps rippled through the crowd.

Harvey sucked in a breath of his own and watched in awe as two griffins and a dragon were led into the ring. An actual *dragon*! He hadn't seen a dragon in any circus for decades, much less one as magnificent as this. The beast's body was roughly the size of one of the elephants that had performed earlier in the night, though with her tail and long neck, she was considerably longer and not quite as bulky. Orange, brown, and cream-colored scales covered her entire body, and each of her toes ended in a giant, hooked claw that could tear a man open in seconds. Thick ropes—presumably enchanted—bound her wings at her sides to keep her from flying off, but Harvey could imagine how powerful and majestic they might be spread out to their full span.

He looked down at his companion. The boy was equally mesmerized, if perhaps for other reasons besides sheer enjoyment of the spectacle. Harvey could practically see the cogs turning in his mind, plotting, scheming. It made him nauseous, but he shook the feeling off as he again turned his attention to the center ring.

The trainer ran the beautiful creatures through a series of increasingly-complex tricks. The griffins leapfrogged over each other in an almost complete circle around the ring, then took turns flying through a metal hoop the dragon held in its jaws. When they weren't performing some trick, they stood regally, eagle eyes surveying the crowd like predators considering their next meal. Their cat-like tails lashed back and forth, and occasionally, they tucked their heads to preen the feathers on their chests and wings.

The trainer placed three metal stools in the center of the ring and directed each beast to stand on one. The center stool looked much too small for the dragon to perch on, but she somehow managed to balance there with ease. All three animals then stood up on their hind legs and clawed at the air before them as if to catch the applause of the delighted crowd.

Harvey smiled in spite of himself. Such magnificent creatures. Seeing a dragon this close made the whole night worthwhile. Or it would have, were it not for his unfortunate part in the events that were sure to come.

The boy elbowed him in the side. "There's our man. Time to go introduce yourself."

"Can't it wait just a few more minutes? The show's almost over, anyway."

"Do I need to remind you why we're here in the first place?"

Harvey sighed and reluctantly donned his fedora. "Where is he, then?"

"By the entrance, the tall man in the cowboy hat."

He spotted the man standing with crossed arms near the end of the big top. His eyes were shadowed under the wide brim of his hat, but he was younger than Harvey had expected, probably in his mid-twenties. His worn blue jeans and muddy boots would have been more appropriate attire for one of the circus' workmen than for its owner.

"Are you sure that's him?" he asked the boy.

"Absolutely. He looks just like his old man. Let's go."

Harvey stood and led the way, apologizing to those he walked in front of as he went. When he reached the end of the big top, he glanced back to make sure the boy was right behind him. He was, and they approached the man in the cowboy hat together.

"Excuse me, sir," Harvey said. "You wouldn't happen to be Mr. Jacob Strickland, would you?"

The man stood up a little straighter. "Call me Jake. How can I help you folks?"

"It's such an honor to meet you. This is a phenomenal show you have here. Absolutely phenomenal."

"I really appreciate that, Mr.—"

"Oh, pardon me. Malone. Harvey Malone. And this young man is my grandson."

Strickland nodded to the boy. "Pleasure to meet you both."

"Likewise," Harvey replied. "I regret that we have to leave before the show's over, but when I saw you, I just had to come and introduce myself. I'm so impressed with everything I've seen here. Frankly, I haven't seen a show this incredible since I was a boy."

"That's awful kind of you," Strickland said, "but I can't take credit for that. We're lucky to have such talented performers."

"Oh, you're too modest. I'm sure it takes a great deal of skill and intelligence to manage all this. I'm impressed, truly." He pulled a small, cream-colored card from his pocket and handed it to the circus owner. "Listen, I run several businesses in Ravington and the surrounding area, and I'm always looking for new opportunities to invest. If that's ever something you'd be interested in for your show, you let me know. All my information is on that card."

Strickland glanced at the business card and stuck it in his back pocket. "I will. Thanks for coming out to see us."

Harvey grinned and shook the man's hand. "Oh, I wouldn't have missed it for anything in the world." He glanced down at the boy beside him. "Ready to go?"

"Yes, Grandpa." There was only a slight sting of contempt in his voice.

They exited the tent and stepped into the cool evening air. Harvey set out across the circus lot at a brisk pace, and even though his companion had to hurry to keep up with his longer strides, he didn't slow down.

"You remember what to do when he contacts you, right?"

Harvey nodded. "As long as the magic in that card works like you say it will."

"Don't you worry about that. He's forgotten us already. The memory enchantment will activate once he gets desperate, so all you have to do now is wait. If he has any more good sense than his father, you may not even have to lift a finger."

Harvey wasn't sure which outcome he should hope for.

They walked in silence for a few minutes, and as they went, he could almost feel the magic of the circus fading away. Maybe it had just been his own delusion all along, but he no longer felt like a decades-younger man. Age settled back into his bones like rust on iron, and the farther they got from the big top, the more intensely guilt gnawed at his thoughts.

When he couldn't take it anymore, he spoke up. "Are you sure this is the only way?"

The boy laughed. The dissonance between the snide maturity in the sound and the childish tone created by the body that uttered it was unnerving in the dark. "Of course it isn't. But this is the best way, which is why we're doing it."

"I just thought, maybe you don't have to…." He stopped himself, suddenly remembering who he was talking to. "Well, never mind."

The boy sighed. "Look, pops, I don't need you telling me how to run my business, okay? Do your part, and all your problems go away, just like we talked about. It's that simple."

"Of course."

They kept walking, and as the last sounds of the circus faded away behind them, Harvey tried to stifle the quiet voice of his conscience, whispering that he had just brought about the destruction of something incredible.

# CHAPTER 1

## THE DRAGON'S ESCAPE

By the time Jake donned his hat and exited his private sleeper car to greet the day, the rosy glow of dawn was already fading, the train cars had all been unloaded, and bright-eyed townies stood by chattering eagerly amongst themselves as they waited for the parade to begin.

He'd slept later than he'd meant to. The tracks on this stretch of the show's route were rough, and the constant jostling had aggravated his three-year-old spinal injury, making sleep almost impossible. Normally, he'd ask Grace for something to curb the pain, but after their most recent argument, he wasn't quite ready to go sulking through the troupers' sleeper cars to beg for her forgiveness.

Too proud and too stubborn for his own good, just like Ma always used to tell him. If he'd picked a bad time to dig up an old dispute with the one person who could help him, he only had himself to blame.

The parade was already lined up, and Jake made his way toward the front of the procession. Bruno sat atop the gilded red ticket wagon, its sides emblazoned with bold lettering that spelled out *Strickland's Circus*. He wore the iconic top hat and red suit of a circus announcer, and he motioned for Jake to hurry up with a white-gloved hand.

Jake broke into a jog, trying to ignore the pain that lanced up his back with each footfall. He hoisted himself up onto the wagon beside his friend and took the reins.

"I'm glad you could finally join us this morning," Bruno said with a mischievous twinkle in his eyes. "Late night?"

Jake grunted. "Not for the reasons you're suggesting."

The dwarf raised one thick eyebrow. "I take it you still haven't resolved your little lovers' quarrel, then?"

"Are we ready to go?"

Bruno chuckled at his avoidance of the question and snapped the reins. "Yes, I believe so."

The pair of draft horses hitched to the wagon shook their manes and started forward. Behind them, the band struck up a lively marching tune, and the townies cheered as the procession of wagons, animals, and costumed troupers made its way to the performance lot.

Bruno passed the reins to Jake and stood up on the bench, one hand atop the wagon for balance as he waved to the onlookers with the other. A natural showman, as always. His beaming smile was contagious, and the townies grinned and waved back at him without even seeming to notice Jake.

That was just fine by him. It was his show, but he'd never much liked the idea of being the public face of Strickland's Circus.

It didn't take long to reach the lot less than a mile away from the train yard. When they did, Jake passed the reins back to Bruno and hopped off the still-moving wagon to survey the area. It was a decent spot for a show, and one they'd performed at many times before. The surrounding area was less populated than some of their stops farther east, and according to the notes in his father's old route book, ticket sales had been inconsistent the last several years. Some seasons, the show was sold out. Others, they barely sold enough tickets to justify making the stop at all. Hopefully, today would bear a closer resemblance to the former.

Tents for the animals had already been raised, as had the cookhouse, menagerie, and performers' dressing tent. The roustabouts had just started working on the big top. They unloaded wagons and carried poles and canvas to their designated locations while sledge gangs hammered stakes into the ground in a perfectly-timed rhythm of clanging metal.

Jake started toward the menagerie to check on the arrangements inside. A voice from behind sent his heart lurching into his stomach and stopped him in his tracks.

"Jake, wait a minute."

He turned around to face Grace. Her lips were pursed and downturned at the corners, and she wouldn't meet his gaze. When she got to him, she simply reached into the bag slung across her chest and pulled out a small vial of clear, purple liquid, which she held out. "It was a pretty rough ride last night, and I know how your back gets, so I figured...well, anyway, you don't have to take it if you don't need it."

His fingers brushed against hers as he accepted the potion, and he squelched the nervous fluttering in his stomach as he held the vial up for closer examination. "There ain't as much as usual."

"You mentioned it hasn't been working well lately, so I'm trying something new. There's less, but it's more concentrated. Hopefully that will help."

"Hopefully." He opened the vial and downed its contents in one swallow. It slid down his throat like sludge and didn't taste much better, but the electric sensation in his back immediately began to subside. "Thank you."

She glanced up at him from beneath long, dark lashes. "Anytime."

A stifling silence lingered in the air between them.

This wasn't how it was supposed to be. This wasn't them. The tension had only started because of some stupid, repeat argument about Jake's father. Stubbornness and personal pride be damned, he couldn't let the man keep ruining his life from beyond the grave.

He took half a step closer to her. "I'm sorry."

"Me too."

Jake shook his head. "You've got nothing to apologize for. I shouldn't have said the things that I did, and I shouldn't have stormed off like that."

She glanced down and fidgeted with the hem of her shirt, not saying anything. After a few seconds, her lips turned up in a small, sly smirk. "Well, you *were* pretty awful."

"The worst," he agreed.

"The *worst* of the worst."

He laughed. "I said I was sorry. You gonna forgive me, or what?"

She narrowed her eyes at him as she pretended to deliberate his request. "Fine, I guess you're forgiven. But you owe me."

"Is that right?" He wrapped an arm around her waist and pulled her close. Her breath tickled the skin on his neck as he leaned forward to whisper in her ear. "Owe you what?"

"I haven't decided yet. You'll just have to wait and see."

He brushed her long, dark hair out of her face, but her eyes shifted to something behind him before he could kiss her. Her brows drew together in concern, and Jake turned to see what had caught her attention.

A trio of men led by Otto Hobbs jogged toward them. Otto's beet-red face was scrunched up tight, and the two men behind him looked equally distressed. Something must have gone wrong with the animals. The only question was just how big a problem it was.

Otto came to a stop in front of Jake, breathless and sputtering. "She's gone, boss. Took off before we could stop her. It's my fault. The boys told me it was too soon for Jeremiah to work with the old girl, him being a First of May and all. But did I listen? Of course not."

It was hard to keep up with Otto's brisk, clipped speech. He talked fast under normal circumstances, but even more so when he was nervous, and delivering bad news made him nervous. So did lying.

"Slow down," Jake said. "What happened?"

Otto barely seemed to hear him as he continued his rant. "I figured the lad's had more than enough time to learn how to get a dragon off the train and into her wagon. Foolish, I realize now, but with us being down a few men and the parade about to start, I was just trying to keep things running smoothly, see? But he got a little too close on her blind side and spooked her. She scared the living daylights out of the other men with her snarling and snapping, then she ran off. I'm sorry, Jake. I should have known better." He dabbed at the sweat on his brow with a greasy handkerchief, his eyes shifting nervously. "I don't think she could have gone far. I was hoping you or Grace could help us get her back? You both have such a knack with her, and it would be a lot easier if you came with us. That is, if it's not too much trouble."

He knew better than to let just anyone work with Calico Thunder. Jake suspected the real story was that one of the more inexperienced men under Otto's supervision had decided he could handle the dragon only to realize too late that he was woefully mistaken. But Otto had always been fiercely protective of his crew, often taking the heat for their mistakes to shield them from the consequences. As long as he kept them in line—and he did, for the most part—Jake was content to play along.

This wasn't the first time Calico Thunder had gotten loose, and while it wasn't something Jake encouraged, it wasn't necessarily a *bad* thing, either. In fact, it could work in their favor, so long as they found her before she could do too much damage. "Which way did she go?"

"She ran off toward town," Otto replied. "I sent one of my boys after her with the truck, but considering the state she was in when she left, it's going to take more than our coaxing to get her back here."

"You want me to grab some of her special potion?" Grace asked. "I think I still have a jar or two from the last batch."

Jake nodded. "Sounds like we're gonna need it."

♦ ♦ ♦

They followed the truck's tracks and the directions of a few helpful locals who'd seen Calico Thunder charge by until they eventually reached a small pig farm on the outskirts of town. The dragon sat on her haunches just outside a wood-slat fence, the fresh carcass of a young pig pinned under one clawed foreleg. An irate man—presumably the pig farmer—shouted at the roustabout who'd driven the truck, but neither of them seemed willing to risk getting any closer to Calico Thunder in the middle of her meal.

Jake approached the two men, Otto just a few steps behind him, and raised a hand to the farmer in greeting. "Good morning. I see our dragon's been stirring up some trouble."

"Trouble?" the farmer raged. "*Trouble* is when one of my hogs escapes the pen and goes missing. This is a disaster!"

"I understand, sir, and I'm sorry about your animal. How can I make it up to you? Name your price."

The man stopped fuming, and his scowl became one of contemplation rather than anger. He scratched at the stubble on his jaw with dirt-coated fingers. "Well, a hog like that, that age, that size—he would have been worth at least fifty dollars."

Jake turned to Calico Thunder and took another look at the mangled pig carcass. It couldn't have even been half grown yet, and it certainly wasn't worth the full fifty dollars the farmer had claimed. But if that was all it took to set the man at ease, he was more than willing to pay.

He took out his billfold and counted the money, then handed it over along with four tickets to the circus. "For your trouble. If you can find it in your heart to forgive the old girl, maybe you'd like to come to the show today and see her in the ring. I reckon you'll find her more entertaining when she's not eating your livestock."

The farmer chuckled a little as he stuck the money and the tickets in his pocket.

Otto handed Jake a small jar filled with an opaque yellow substance. "I'll get the truck ready," he said and hurried to back it up into a more suitable position.

Jake turned away from the farmer and opened the jar. He tried not to inhale through his nose, but he still caught a whiff of the acrid substance and gagged. Calico Thunder caught the scent, too. She stopped in the middle of tearing another strip of flesh from her pig and turned her broad head to Jake. The muscles in her back twitched, and the enchanted ropes binding her wings to her sides stretched a little as she shifted to scratch under her belly with one rear foot.

He advanced at a steady pace, staying within line-of-sight of her one good, golden-yellow eye. The other had turned milky white from a cataract long before Jake had joined the circus, and the old girl tended to get annoyed when people snuck up on her from her blind spot.

She let out a low, rumbling growl as he came closer, but it wasn't the threatening kind. Most people couldn't tell the difference, but he'd spent enough time around dragons—and this one in particular—to know what was a warning and what was just talk. Didn't mean he ever let his guard down completely, but he liked to think they had a bond of sorts, some kind of mutual understanding. They were kindred spirits, both former rodeo headliners who'd somehow wound up on a traveling circus train and found a way to make it work.

He stopped at her side and ran a hand over her scaly hide, a mottled pattern of white, orange, and dark brown that had earned her her moniker. Beneath the scales, every inch of her body was pure muscle. Her jaws could crush a man's ribcage with little effort, and one swing from her spiked tail could knock him down and send him skidding across the ground with at least a few broken bones.

But he wasn't afraid. Careful, always, but not afraid. She'd never snapped at him like she did some of the others, and besides, she'd never actually bitten anyone. She was just good at warning those she didn't like to steer clear.

"I hope you enjoyed your meal, old girl," he said, patting her shoulder. "Cost us a small fortune, but I guess you've earned a little fine dining, haven't you?"

Calico Thunder snorted and attempted to push her snout into the jar he held.

"Come on then. Let's get going." He took a few steps back and began giving her commands in a strong, authoritative tone. "Up! Come on, up!"

She wasn't in the ring, and she gave Jake a look of annoyance at being asked to follow orders outside of show time. After a few seconds, she complied, standing up on all four legs and waiting for her next command.

"Come," he said.

She took one long stride forward, then another. Jake kept moving back, and she followed. She was surprisingly willing to leave her meal, thanks to Grace's potion. The mixture was some sort of mild dragon intoxicant, and even when she was at her most difficult, Calico Thunder couldn't resist the bribe.

They eventually made it to the truck, and Jake reached through the bars of the cage enclosing its bed and set the jar in the back corner. Once she was at the open door, he tapped his hand twice against the wood floor. "Step up."

She raised one foreleg and put it inside, then the other. The truck creaked under her weight as she maneuvered through the door and stretched herself out on the floor. Once settled, she stuck her long, forked tongue into the jar to lap up its rancid, milky contents.

Jake turned back to Otto and the roustabout, who was bent over near the fence where Calico Thunder had been standing. He was turning something over in his hand. It was hard to tell for sure from this distance, but it looked like the old, discarded top layer of a dragon scale.

The roustabout caught Jake's eye as he stood up and sheepishly shoved the item into his pocket.

Jake pretended he hadn't noticed and pointed to the half-eaten pig carcass. "Grab the rest of that and throw it in with her." It was good meat, and he'd already paid for it. No sense in leaving it behind.

He approached the farmer, who had watched the whole affair with his mouth agape, and reached out to shake the man's hand. "Again, I'm real sorry about all this. At least you'll have a good story to tell your neighbors. Ain't every day a dragon shows up right in your backyard."

The farmer scratched at his bald head. "No, I suppose it isn't."

"We'll get out of your way, then. Hope to see you at the show tonight."

"I wouldn't miss it."

Jake smiled as he turned away from the man and returned to the truck. He sat in the passenger seat and let Otto drive with the roustabout scrunched in the middle between them.

As they rumbled down the dirt road to head back to the circus lot, the roustabout turned to Jake. "Um…Mr. Strickland, sir? Can I ask you a question?"

"Sure."

"Why didn't you ask that farmer to keep quiet about all this? I mean, isn't it a *bad* thing that Calico Thunder took off like that?"

"It ain't something I encourage, but we have to work with what we've got. The show must go on, after all."

"Sure, but an escaped dragon? Isn't that going to scare people off?"

"Just the opposite, actually." He'd make back every penny he'd paid for that pig and more by the time the night was over. Posters and billboards and parades were fine, but there was no better advertising than word of mouth. "Everyone likes having a good story to tell. You wait and see. Before noon, townies will be lining up at the ticket booth just to get a glimpse of the dragon who poached their neighbor's livestock."

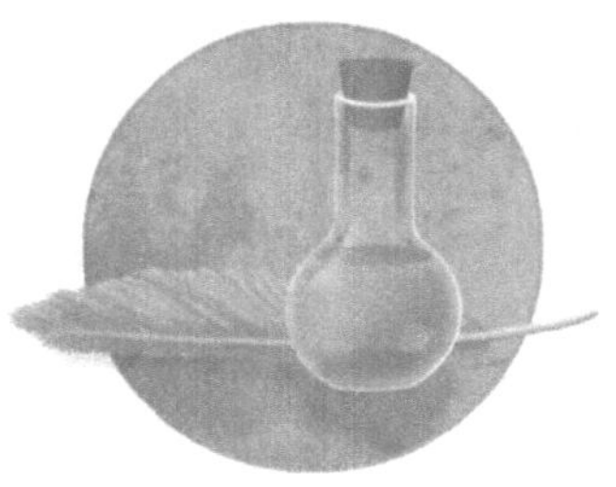

# CHAPTER 2

## AN IMPOSSIBLE DEBT

Once they made it back to the lot, Jake helped Otto and his men get Calico Thunder settled into her enclosure inside the ring stock tent, where she would stay until it was time for her performance under the big top. For the next fifteen minutes, he lectured the animal caretakers on proper transport procedures and forbid the inexperienced workman who'd been responsible for the dragon's escape from ever going near her again. Her escapades made for good, easy advertising from time to time, but any more than that could ruin the circus' reputation just as easily.

The men trudged out of the tent one by one. Otto lagged behind with Jake to watch them go. "Sorry again for the trouble. They're good boys, and it really was my fault."

"I doubt that, but I'm sure they appreciate you saying so."

Otto grunted and headed outside, probably to give the men a lecture of his own before they fed and watered the rest of the animals.

Jake made his way over to Grace, who tended to her griffins at the other end of the tent. He took stock of all the other animals as he passed by, mentally checking off which ones were already in their enclosures. He walked past the unicorns and hippogriffs, the brightly colored wyverns, the horses and elephants, and the family of golden-red phoenixes sitting on their perch. Each one would dazzle the audience later that day during the circus' two shows, but none quite so much as Grace and her extraordinary winged beasts. Or at least, that was what Jake liked to think, but he was admittedly biased.

She was still cooing to the griffins when he reached her. The larger of the two, Trigger, nuzzled her hand with his curved beak while his brother Bullseye preened the copper-colored feathers of his wings. Jake leaned over the fence to stroke Trigger's neck.

"Hey there, cowboy," Grace said.

He smiled at the old pet name. It was something she'd taken to calling him when he first came to help his dad with the circus three years ago. That seemed like ancient history now. A lot had changed since then, but some things just stuck.

He nodded to the griffins. "They seem content this morning."

"Well, they just came back from a long walk outside, so they should be." Trigger gently tugged at strands of her dark hair with his beak, and she laughed. For a moment, Jake wanted to reach out and run his fingers through the long, loose waves himself, but he resisted the impulse.

She glanced over at Calico Thunder. "I see you brought our girl back safe and sound."

"It wasn't too hard, thanks to that disgusting concoction of yours." He shook his head and pretended to shudder. "I can never get over how *bad* that stuff smells."

"Try making it sometime. I swear the scent is stuck in my nostrils for days afterward."

"I think I'll just leave that delightful task to you."

She shoved his arm. "Scoundrel."

"I never claimed to be anything else."

She clicked her tongue at the griffins and gave them each a scratch under the chin. "I'm hungry. Do you think the flag's up yet?"

"Should be. You wanna head over?"

"Sure."

They exited the tent hand in hand and were halfway to the cookhouse when Otto came running up to them again. Jake sighed. *What now?*

"Some men are at the ticket booth asking to see you," he said breathlessly. "Fancy types—expensive suits, flashy watches.

"They say what they want?"

"No. Just that it's important."

Grace gave his hand a squeeze. "I'll make sure the cooks save you some food."

"Thanks." He changed course for the ticket booth. An impressively long line of townies had already started to form in front, even though they wouldn't be letting anyone in for another hour at least. Maybe word of Calico Thunder's morning escape had already started to spread.

The men Otto had spoken of stood apart from the rest, conspicuous in their pinstripe suits, stiff-collared shirts, and wingtip shoes devoid of so much as a speck of dirt. There were three of them, two of whom were massive ogres with hulking frames, fiery eyes, and long fangs protruding over their upper lips. The third man was human and appeared to be about the same height as Jake, but between his two companions, he looked abnormally small. The gold chain of a pocket watch draped across the dark vest under his suit jacket.

Jake strode toward them. "Can I help you gentlemen?"

The human man raised an eyebrow. "Mr. Strickland?"

"Yessir. What can I do for you?"

"We did some business with your father a few years back, and we're just here to follow up on that. Do you mind if we take a walk?"

Jake had met most of Cliff's business contacts over the past three years, but he couldn't remember seeing any of these men before. "What did you say your name was?"

The man stuck his hands in his pockets. "I assume you're just as eager to get back to the rest of your day as I am. Shall we find somewhere more private to discuss this?"

Why wouldn't he just answer the question? What was he hiding? Jake might have turned them all away, but the threatening way the two ogres eyed him indicated the request wasn't open for discussion. He followed their lead as they started down a narrow dirt road leading to the train yard, away from the ticket booth and any prying eyes that might have been there.

The ogres fell behind, leaving Jake alone beside the third man. No one said anything for a minute or two, but once they'd left the gathering crowd of townies behind, the man cleared his throat. "Let's talk business, shall we, Jake? It is Jake, isn't it?"

"Yes. But like you said, I've got other work to get back to, so I'd appreciate if you could get right to the point."

A toothy smile peered out from beneath the man's mustache. "Of course. Your father was always a very direct man—never wanted to waste any time. I respect that. As I said earlier, I'm actually here because of him. You see, Cliff owed me a rather significant amount of money. I understand he's gone now, and I hate to put this on you, but unfortunately, I can't just ignore a debt like this. Someone has to take responsibility."

Jake frowned. He'd paid all his father's outstanding debts—of which there had been many—when he took over the circus after Cliff's death. It was possible something had slipped through the cracks, but it was also possible this was just a scam. The three men looked respectable enough, but they still hadn't told him their names, and besides that, there was something *off* about them. Something Jake couldn't quite pinpoint, but it made him wary all the same.

"You got proof?" he asked.

"Of course." The man reached inside his suit jacket and pulled out a set of folded papers. He spread them open before passing them over.

Jake scanned each page of what appeared to be a contract signed and dated five years prior. He recognized his father's messy signature scrawled across the bottom of the last page. The second signature, clear and distinct, read 'Vincent A. Burke.'

"Vincent Burke? Is this some kind of joke?" He looked up with narrowed eyes. "Who are you?"

The man smirked. His facial features shifted, and a few seconds later, Jake was no longer staring at the unremarkable bearded gentleman he'd met at the ticket booth. This man was cleanshaven, with green eyes, dark hair, and a smile too wide for his face—a face Jake had seen in dozens of newspapers from the Midwest to the East Coast.

Vincent Burke, high-profile Viterian mobster and one of the nation's most wanted criminals.

Burke had only dropped his glamour for a few seconds before he conjured up the false appearance once more. The illusion was an effective disguise and helped to explain how he'd managed to evade arrest on multiple occasions and escape prison whenever he was captured. The man had become a legend over the last few years, and now that legend was standing right in front of Jake talking about an old business deal he'd made with his father. He gaped.

"You'll want to take a look at that contract again," Burke said.

Jake fumbled through the pages. When his eyes fell on the amount his father owed, his stomach plummeted. "You missin' a decimal point in there somewhere?"

Burke shook his head. "I'm afraid not. Four hundred thousand dollars. You understand why I can't just let it go."

He stopped walking and silently cursed his father. Even in death, Cliff continued to let him down.

"I don't have that kind of money," he said. "I'm struggling to get by every month as it is, and I've gotta take care of the animals and my employees first. I'd be happy to work out some kind of installment plan to repay the debt." Not that it would do much good. Even if he gave Burke every penny he earned—minus the circus' expenses—he'd be making payments until the day they put his body in the ground.

Burke clicked his tongue. "I might have been willing to work something out before. After all, Cliff used to be pretty good about making his payments on time—wasn't he, boys?" The two ogres nodded, and Burke went on. "Unfortunately, we haven't been getting anything for the past three years. I tried to contact him multiple times to remind him of our arrangement, but I never got a response. I'm afraid I can't afford to wait any longer."

"My father was real sick. I'm sure that's why he didn't pay you. I would have sent the money after I took over if I'd known, but this is the first time I'm hearing anything about it."

Why hadn't his father ever said anything about this? Or had Jake just missed it somehow? There had been *so* much paperwork to go through after Cliff died. He'd owed money to a lot of people, but all combined, those debts didn't even come close to matching this one.

"I understand, of course," Burke said sympathetically, "but business is business. We're going to need that money by the end of the month."

The request was so ridiculous Jake might have laughed were it not for the two massive ogres looming over him and the perfectly sober expression on Burke's face. "I told you, I'm scraping by here. I just don't have that much money."

Burke's eyebrows settled low over his eyes. "Then I suggest you find it soon, because you're not going to like what happens if you don't." He started walking down the road again.

Jake stood frozen for another moment, then scrambled to catch up with him. "You can't do this. It's extortion. I'll contact the police."

Burke stopped and turned around slowly. His glamour was gone, and the face that stared back at Jake—his true face—bore an expression as hard and cold as a frozen lake. "I wouldn't do that, if I were you," he said flatly. "I've had men killed for lesser threats. Haven't I, Sean?"

"You have," said the shorter of the two ogres. He laid a heavy hand on Jake's shoulder and squeezed. "Do you want me to show him?"

A hard knot formed in Jake's chest. What had he been thinking, talking to a dangerous criminal like that? He should have kept his stupid mouth shut. Once Burke left, he could figure out a plan, but for now, he just needed to avoid pissing him off. "I'm sorry."

Burke cocked his head to the side and flashed his unnaturally wide grin again. "Thank you. I know this is all a shock to you, so I'll make an exception for your disrespectful comments. But in all seriousness, Jake, contacting the authorities would be *very* unwise. You understand that, don't you? You're a smart man. I mean, you don't honestly believe the cops are going to help you. Not with all the money the Viterian mob puts in their pockets."

He shook his head. "No, of course not. It was stupid. Look, can we all just take a step back here and start over? I'm sure we can come up with a compromise."

The mobster's eyes narrowed in thoughtful consideration. "Hmm. Well, I suppose there *is* something we could arrange. A trade, for instance. If you gave me the circus, I'd be willing to forget all about your father's debt."

"What? No—I can't do that."

"Why not? From what I understand, it's been more of a burden to you than a blessing. Let me take it off your hands."

He wasn't wrong, and for the briefest moment, Jake let himself entertain the idea. How freeing would it be not to have to worry about expenses and profit margins anymore? To sleep peacefully at night instead of tossing and turning, wondering if he'd even have enough to pay everyone each month. Especially now, knowing he owed four hundred thousand dollars to the Viterian mob. How was he ever going to pay that back?

He didn't have the answer yet, but handing over the circus wasn't it. He couldn't do that to Grace or Bruno or any of the other dedicated men and women for whom the circus was home. "I'm sorry, but I just can't. There's gotta be something else we can work out."

Burke clicked his tongue and shook his head disapprovingly. "I still don't think you understand who you're dealing with." His eyes flicked over to Sean, who reached forward and seized Jake by the collar of his shirt. The ogre lifted him off the ground as easily as he might have lifted a small child. Jake's hat fell into the dust, and he kicked the empty air in a desperate attempt to free himself.

Burke took a few slow steps forward and stared up at him. "This is not a negotiation. Your father owed the Viterian mob, and since you run his business now, that's on you. If you don't like it, you can take it up with him when you meet him in Hell, because that's exactly where you're headed if you don't have our money the next time we show up. You and all your other little friends on this show. Do I make myself abundantly clear?"

Jake sucked in a sputtering breath as images of all the things he wanted to do and say to Burke and his lackeys ran through his mind. If he were any younger or less mature—and if he weren't currently dangling two feet above the ground—he might have fired back with some brazen retort that would have only provoked Burke's anger even further. He might have even tried to punch the man for threatening him like that. He would have fought all three of them with no regard for the consequences, and he would have taken a serious beating for it while accomplishing nothing.

Now he was smart enough to know when to back down, so he just nodded.

Sean released him. He fell to the ground and bit back a groan as pain shot up his spine like lightning. Trying to preserve what little dignity he had left, he forced himself to stand.

"I'm glad we could come to an understanding," Burke said. He motioned to the second ogre, who picked up the fallen cowboy hat, dusted it off, and returned it to Jake's head. "But just in case, I've decided to leave Clarence with you for the next few weeks. We wouldn't want you getting any ideas about running off and disappearing on us. I expect you to show him the utmost hospitality."

Clarence smiled down at Jake, but the razor-sharp teeth lined between his protruding fangs made it look more like a snarl.

Burke motioned for Sean to follow him, and they headed down the road that would take them to the trainyard. Without looking back, the mobster raised a hand over his shoulder in a goodbye wave. "It's been a pleasure, Jake. See you next month."

# CHAPTER 3

## SINS OF THE FATHER

Jake made his way to the cookhouse with Clarence's enormous shadow looming over him like his very own personal storm cloud. His appetite had vanished somewhere along the road back to the lot, but he grabbed the plate the cooks had saved for him anyway and sat next to Grace and Bruno at a table on the performer's side of the tent.

The ogre joined them a minute later, his plate piled so high that food was starting to spill off the edges. When he sat down with a heavy *thunk*, he nearly sent Bruno flying. The dwarf wasn't even half Clarence's size, but he shot him a dirty look anyway before turning back to his meal. Clarence didn't seem to notice.

Jake stared down at his food absently until Grace kicked his leg under the table. He blinked away the clamor of anxious thoughts fighting for his attention, and she tilted her head in Clarence's direction with a curious expression.

Jake shoved a forkful of potatoes into his mouth to buy himself a few seconds. The ogre was going to be hanging around for the next several weeks, so he might as well make introductions, but what was he supposed to say? He couldn't tell them the truth. At least not here, surrounded by everyone else. He had enough to worry about already, and dragging the entire circus into it would only make things worse.

"This is Clarence," he said after gulping down some water from a tin cup. "He's an old friend of mine. From the rodeo. He'll be traveling with us for a few weeks, wants to see what circus life is like."

Grace raised her eyebrows, clearly not buying any of it, but she was tactful enough not to press the issue.

Bruno, however, was not. "The rodeo, huh? And what exactly did you do in the rodeo?"

Clarence wiped gravy from his face with the back of his hand and flashed Bruno his sharp, fang-toothed smile. "Clown."

Bruno scowled. "The stuff of nightmares. Children must have loved you."

Clarence let out a deep, throaty laugh. "The dwarf makes jokes. Are you a clown, too?"

His barrel chest puffed out, and his eyes sparked like firecrackers beneath his bushy eyebrows. "I most certainly am not! I—"

"Bruno," Grace interrupted. "I had a new idea for introducing my act I wanted to go over with you. Are you done eating?"

Some of his anger dissipated as he turned to her. "Yes, of course, dear. I'm sure these two gentlemen have a lot of catching up to do."

Jake nodded his thanks as she stood up from the table, but she only stared at him with pursed lips. No doubt he'd hear about this later, but at least now he had a few minutes to mull over his predicament without having to hide his internal panic from the two people who knew him best.

How on earth was he supposed to come up with four hundred thousand dollars in a month?

The question circled his thoughts over and over again as he stabbed at his food and forced himself to eat. He still didn't have any answers for that question, but his mind soon provided him with a new one.

How had his father gotten into this mess in the first place?

That was a much easier question, and one he had a lifetime's worth of answers for.

Cliff Strickland had been nearly as irresponsible in his management of the circus as he had been in his role as a father. He'd come and gone sporadically throughout Jake's childhood, leaving him and his mother to fend for themselves most of the time while he went off chasing dreams of wealth and fame in the circus. On the rare nights he was home, he used to tell Jake stories about flying acrobats, prancing unicorns, and fearless griffin tamers. And dragons. Big, ferocious, powerful dragons with teeth like spearheads and scales as hard as stone.

It was the stories of dragons that had driven Jake to show business when he was sixteen, old enough to fend for himself, but still too young to recognize the exaggeration in his father's tales. By that time, he resented Cliff enough that pride wouldn't allow him to join the circus—any circus—but the idea of working with the majestic dragons he'd heard so much about was too good to resist. He joined up with the first wild west show that would have him.

By seventeen, he'd ridden his first dragon in the arena before a pitifully small audience, an experience every bit as thrilling as he'd imagined. By eighteen, he was making enough money to send some to Ma every month. By twenty, she was dead. And by twenty-three, Jake's career was over, broken along with his spine after a bad ride left him lying in the dirt under the legs of a four-ton dragon.

The doctors and magical Healers did their best, but they all said the same thing in the end. He was lucky to even be walking, and riding dragons again was out of the question. When the last letter from his father came in the form of an offer to work on the circus, Jake had no prospects and nothing left to lose. He boarded a train the next day and resigned himself to a life he'd never wanted.

Things were already bad for the show when he arrived. Cliff had always been a dreamer, and the practical realities of running a business could never compete with his fantastical ideas of what the circus should be. When he got sick, he turned desperate, taking up a frantic quest to secure his legacy and turn Strickland's Circus into the greatest show on earth. He bought more exotic animals than he could possibly hope to care for and hired more performers than he could possibly hope to pay. He nearly ran his business into bankruptcy, and then he died and left the whole mess to Jake to sort out.

Hard to feel grateful for an inheritance when it came with more trouble than it was worth from a man who'd never given him anything he needed before.

Over the next two years, Jake had worked hard to turn the circus into a profitable business once more. He'd cut the menagerie in half and fired at least a third of the performers. Because of that, he'd been able to get away with keeping on just half the working men the next season, and slowly but surely, he began to pay off his father's debts. The show had been operating in the black for barely four months now. It wasn't a huge profit, but Jake took pride in the accomplishment nonetheless.

False pride, he realized now. The debt he owed the mob loomed in his mind, an insurmountable obstacle he could never hope to overcome. But he had to. Somehow, he had to find a way. If not for himself, then for the sake of everyone who depended on the circus for their livelihood.

He crumpled the handkerchief he was using as a napkin in his palm and silently cursed his father. Making a shady business deal with the Viterian mob was one thing, but leaving his son to deal with the fallout and not even having the decency to warn him about it—the man was a real piece of work.

He shouldn't have been surprised. Cliff hadn't given a damn about him when Jake was a kid, so why would things be any different years later? If anything, he should have expected something like this. But he hadn't, and that just pissed him off even more.

Clarence elbowed him in the side and jabbed a thick, stubby finger at his half-eaten meal. "Were you going to finish that?"

He slid the plate across the table. "It's all yours."

The ogre dug in with voracious enthusiasm.

Jake stood up to leave. He'd wasted enough time feeling sorry for himself. There had to be a way out of this mess, but if he was going to find it, he needed to seek the advice of the smartest person he knew. Between him and Grace, they'd figure something out.

"I'll be in the menagerie if you need me," he said to Clarence.

"The menage-what?" The ogre shoveled a last, massive bite into his mouth and spoke between chews. "Hold on a second. Burke told me to keep an eye on you, and that's what I'm going to do. You and I go everywhere together."

"I can't even take a piss in private?" Jake growled.

The ogre's mouth puckered, and he suddenly looked rather embarrassed. "Of course you can, but...I just need to know where you are."

He sighed. Having this giant shadow lurking behind him all day was going to get old fast. But the ogre had to sleep sometime. He could wait until tonight to talk to Grace.

"Come on, then." He left the cookhouse with Clarence lumbering along behind him. "Let's go find ourselves something to do. If you're gonna be here all month, you're gonna work. No one eats for free on this show. Not even the mob."

# CHAPTER 4

## MIDNIGHT RENDEZVOUS

The two shows the troupers performed later that day were as good as Jake could have possibly hoped for. Bruno was a perfect showman, rousing the audience's enthusiasm for each act with his booming gusto and charisma. Grace, Trigger, and Bullseye were crowd favorites as usual, but the real star of the show was Calico Thunder. News of her venture to the pig farm had spread, and the audience cheered with delight when she entered the center ring. Even Madame Arabella, the circus' renowned illusionist, didn't get as much applause as the dragon.

Ordinarily, Jake would have been thrilled to see so many happy faces in the stands. Tonight, all he could think about was how small a dent those ticket sales would make in the massive sum he owed Burke. Selling more tickets and playing more shows was not the solution to his problem, but he was still no closer to figuring out what was.

Later that night, while the train clattered along the tracks on its way to their next destination, he lay awake listening to Clarence's heavy snores. The ogre had been asleep for a solid fifteen minutes now. It was as good a time as any to go find Grace, but he couldn't seem to force himself out of bed. She wasn't going to react well to the news he had for her.

He gave himself a few more seconds, then sat up with a sigh and pulled on his boots. Tiptoeing past Clarence, he headed to the back of the train car and carefully opened the door. The muffled rumble of the wheels became a roar, but Clarence didn't stir. Jake stepped out into the night and slid the door shut behind him.

The tracks rushed by in a blur of shadows below the small platform he now stood on. He stepped across the gap to the next car and opened the door. A hot, musty, animal smell hit him in the face, and the hippogriffs stirred in their pens. A similar smell greeted him through several more stock cars. When he reached the one that housed Trigger, Bullseye, and Calico Thunder, the scent was a little more rank, mixed with the remains of the goat and chickens that had been their supper. Jake didn't mind. He'd spent enough time around animals to find the smell almost comforting. He preferred their company to most peoples', even with the stink.

He braced himself for the clamor he knew would greet him before opening the next door. A dozen or so performers sat on their bunks in a makeshift circle, playing cards and laughing uproariously in the light of a hanging lantern. A few more slept, or at least tried to.

The noise died down a little when they spotted him, and he searched for Grace's face among theirs. She met his gaze from a top bunk near the rear end of the car. After excusing herself from the game, she hopped down and sauntered toward him. There were a few wolf-whistles and lewd comments as she passed, then more laughter when Jake bowed his head to hide the blush spreading across his cheeks.

Grace just laughed with the rest of them. Their romance was no secret among the troupers, but Jake tried to maintain some measure of discretion where he could. Grace, on the other hand, couldn't care less. He would never come to the performers' bunk car seeking her out for some late-night company, but she'd been known to venture to his car in the early hours of the morning from time to time.

She looped her arm through his and winked dramatically over her shoulder at the others, which only riled them up even further. Then the two of them were out the door and back in the stock car where the dragon and griffins dozed.

"I suppose this means you're ready to tell me what's really going on with that *friend* of yours," she said.

His eyes hadn't quite adjusted to the dark yet, and he couldn't make out her expression. Though, if he had to guess, she was staring at him with crossed arms and the crooked crease between her eyebrows that only appeared when she was angry or worried. By the time they finished talking, she'd probably be both.

"Well?" Grace prodded. "Come on, out with it. You pulled me away from a *very* good hand in there, so whatever it is had better be important."

He stuck his hands in his pockets, already bracing himself for her reaction. "You familiar with Vincent Burke?"

She scoffed. "The *mobster*, Vincent Burke? Sure. Who isn't?"

"Did you know my dad did some business with him?"

She hesitated, then softly answered, "I might have. Why?"

"Dammit, Grace. Don't you think that might've been something I needed to know when I took over here?"

"What for? Cliff had already taken care of it. If you'd known, it would have just been another reason for you to hate him."

Jake ran a hand over his face. The man had been dead two years, and she *still* defended his honor like he was some kind of hero. For her, he had been, but Jake would never see him that way. "I don't *hate* him, I just—"

"How did you find out about this anyway?"

"Burke came by the ticket booth today. Apparently, dear old dad didn't *take care of it* after all. Turns out he owed the mob four hundred thousand dollars."

In the dim moonlight filtering between the slats of the train car, Jake could just make out her wide eyes and open mouth. "That can't be right. He never would have—" She stopped and seemed to reconsider what she was about to say. "I didn't realize it was that bad."

"Four hundred thousand dollars. That's almost half a million."

"I know how numbers work, Jake."

"How'd he let that happen?"

"It wasn't like that. It's not his fault."

He shook his head. Of course not. It was *never* his fault. The man was a saint in her eyes, the perfect father figure he had never been to Jake. He clamped his mouth shut to stop himself from hurling that same old, tired argument at her.

Grace must have sensed his frustration. She took a step closer to him and brushed her fingers against his. "That's not what I meant. It's just...he tried, you know. He wasn't perfect, but he tried."

"Well if that's the best he could do, he was a bigger fool than I thought."

She turned to the rough wood boards that fenced in the griffins. Trigger was scratching at the straw restlessly, but he strode over to Grace when she reached out a hand. He nuzzled her outstretched palm with his beak, and her eyes took on a faraway look as she stared back at the griffin. After a few seconds, she reached into her pocket and took out a small, folding knife Jake had seen many times before. The initials *C. S.* were burned into its wood handle.

"Things got pretty bad five, maybe six years ago," she said quietly, turning the knife over and over again in her fingers. "We were broke. Cliff couldn't even keep the animals fed, much less pay everyone, and banks wouldn't loan to him anymore because of all the debt he'd racked up. That's when he asked Burke for help. Strickland's Circus would have been dead if he hadn't."

"He borrowed too much," Jake growled. "And from a man like Burke? What made him think that was a good idea?"

"I doubt he knew who he was dealing with. The Viterians hadn't made much of a name for themselves yet. Back then, Burke was just Burke. He was the last chance Cliff had to save all this, so he took it."

"Anything to hold onto his precious circus." A familiar rage began to simmer inside him. It was the same anger he'd felt at ten years old when Bobby Parker told him his dad was a deadbeat who didn't want him, and again at fifteen when he'd come home to his mom crying over an old family photo. It was the same anger he'd felt after learning he'd never ride dragons again and grudgingly went to work on his father's circus. He'd carried that anger with him his whole life, but that didn't make it any easier to deal with now.

He clenched a fist and shook his head. "It don't matter now. He's been letting me down since I was a kid, so it ain't like anything's changed."

"Is that it?" Grace said. "You're still pissed because he wasn't the perfect father?"

"I'm pissed because he was never a father at all!" The sharpness in his voice elicited a growl from Calico Thunder and a glare from Grace, but he didn't care. "He was never around when I was growing up, and then he dies and decides to throw all this on me. You know, for a while, I actually thought he might be trying to do me some kind of favor. An apology or a peace offering to make up for all the times he wasn't there. Turns out, he was just leaving me another mess to clean up."

Grace didn't say anything, didn't even look at him, but there was a stiffness in her posture like she was trying to hold something in, or maybe just hold herself together.

He shouldn't have shouted. None of this was her fault, and the person he was really angry at wasn't around to hear his frustrations.

He sighed. "I'm sorry. I know he was...different, for you. But you can't expect me to have much forgiveness for the man."

"I don't." She slipped the knife back in her pocket. "Look, none of this is fair, but it is what it is. You can blame Cliff and feel sorry for yourself all you like, but eventually, you're going to have to get past your feelings and *do* something."

She was right, as usual, but he bristled at the comment nonetheless. "I know that."

"Well then, what did Burke say? Were you able to work something out with him?"

"Not exactly. He wants the debt paid in a month."

She stopped running her fingers through Trigger's neck feathers and turned to him. "All of it?"

"All of it. And that ogre, Clarence? He's one of Burke's guys, here to make sure I don't try to run off and disappear or anything like that."

She swore under her breath. "What happens if you can't get the money?"

"Pain was implied. Maybe death. Not just for me, but for everyone on the show."

The crease between Grace's eyebrows deepened. "They can't possibly expect you to come up with that much money in a month."

"That's what I said."

"And?"

"Burke offered to forget about the debt if I turned over the circus." Her mouth dropped in horrified disbelief, and he quickly added, "I turned him down, of course." He left out the terrifying moments he'd spent with his legs dangling above the ground and his shirt collar in Sean's meaty fists. No need to make her worry any more than he already had.

"Why would they even want the circus?"

He shrugged. "I think they just wanna collect the debt however they can get it."

"We'll figure something out," she said, but her voice sounded uncertain.

He took a step closer to her and leaned against the rough wood with his arms dangling over the side. Bullseye lay sprawled out on the ground like a giant cat and lazily opened one amber eye to stare up at him. His tail lashed once, then he went back to sleep.

"I thought about contacting the police."

Grace raised an eyebrow. "Say what you want about Cliff and his hairbrained schemes, but *that* is one of the worst ideas I've ever heard."

Jake chuckled. "I'm a desperate man. I'm willing to try just about anything."

"But the police, cowboy? Seriously? The mob owns the cops in every major city from here to the coast. It's been that way since the Ban. This isn't one of your quaint little towns out west where some honorable sheriff is going to step in and save the day."

"If you've got a better idea, I'd love to hear it."

She resumed stroking Trigger's neck feathers. "You could hold pay for a month. For everyone, not just the roustabouts."

"The performers would never put up with that."

"I think I could make them understand. We might lose a few, starting with Madame Arabella. But you've been dying for a good excuse to let her go, anyway"

That was a fair point. Madame Arabella had been a thorn in his side for months. He'd hired the prima donna illusionist on a year-long contract, and she'd been a strong attraction for the show this season, but sometimes he wondered if her high-strung attitude was worth it. Losing her wouldn't be the worst thing in the world.

He ran a few quick calculations in his head, then sighed. "It's not enough. Not even close. Even if we held pay for months, it wouldn't be enough." Besides that, holding wages for more than a month would cause a mass exodus as performers and roustabouts alike left Strickland's Circus to work on shows where they'd actually make money.

"What if we cut some of the roustabouts loose, too?"

Jake shook his head. "We've got a bare-bones crew as it

is. We might be able to afford cutting a few more, but it wouldn't be enough to make much difference."

Grace chewed on her bottom lip and stared blankly ahead, likely mulling over the same questions that had been running through Jake's head all day. Her talk of laying off some of the working men had sparked another idea, though.

"We could sell some of the animals," he said. "Get rid of their equipment, too. Downsize a little, at least for now."

Grace dug her fingers into Trigger's feathers like she was trying to hold onto him before Jake could take him away. "No. There has to be another way."

"I don't think there is."

"You can't sell the animals. They're family. More importantly, they *are* the circus. Without them, we're just a bunch of misfits on a train."

"I don't like it either, but something's gotta give here. Maybe a little bit of everything. Even then, it won't be enough, but at least it might buy me more time." If he could show Burke and the mob he was doing everything he could to get them their money, maybe they'd reconsider their impossible deadline. But he had to come to them with a substantial offering if he wanted them to take him seriously.

Grace glanced at the door, then looked Jake dead in the eye. "We could kill them." Her voice was little more than a whisper. "First Clarence, then wait until Burke comes to collect and just..." She snapped her fingers. "He disappears. Just like that."

She didn't flinch, didn't even blink, and maybe it was just the darkness, but her eyes were stone-cold. Jake was almost convinced she was actually serious. The circus meant even more to her than it had to his father, and there wasn't much she wouldn't do to save it. Or him.

"This ain't just some street thug peddling charms and jinxes for beer money," he replied. "We do anything to him, and we're asking the entire mob to come after us."

She jostled his shoulder with hers. "Relax, I was joking. I'm not stupid."

They fell silent for a few minutes. The train continued to rumble along the tracks, and Calico Thunder let out a snort from the other side of the car.

"What am I supposed to do?" Jake said at last. He wished she would just tell him. He wished *anyone* would just tell him what to do to make this whole mess go away.

"You'll have to downsize," Grace replied softly.

"But you said—"

She shook her head. "You were right. You'll have to sell some of the menagerie animals, the baggage stock, the equipment. After that, you won't need so many working men, so you can lay off some of them. And you'll probably have to hold pay for the month. For everyone, including the performers. They won't like it, but it's not anything that hasn't happened before. I'll talk to them, make them understand."

It was the only real option he had. He hated that he was in this position, but at least Grace understood. That made it all seem a little less impossible. Losing her respect would have been just about the worst thing he could imagine coming from this whole ordeal.

"I'm sorry," he said.

"For what? This isn't your fault. Your dad was like family to me, but if he were here right now, I'd punch him in the nose myself."

Her perfect image of Cliff had finally been tainted. He shouldn't have taken so much satisfaction in that fact, but he couldn't help himself.

"Just promise me one thing," she said.

"Sure. What's that?"

She nodded to the two griffins who now lay curled up together in the straw. "Don't get rid of my boys here."

"I promise."

A low, growling snort came from behind them, and Grace giggled. "Or Calico Thunder."

Jake glanced over his shoulder at the dragon. Even in sleep, she looked majestically dangerous and beautiful, just like the dragons in the stories his father had told him when he was a boy. He put an arm over Grace's shoulders and pulled her close. "Wouldn't even dream of it."

# CHAPTER 5

## MIRROR TALK

When Jake awoke the next morning, all the stress and anxiety he'd mercifully been able to forget in sleep hit him like an avalanche. For a second, he tried to imagine he'd only dreamed yesterday's nightmare, but that idea was ruined when he saw Clarence's massive foot dangling from the end of the too-small cot where he'd slept.

As he went about getting himself ready for the day, the ogre stirred and sat up. He cracked his neck a few times, stretched his burly limbs, and flashed one of his pointy smiles. "Good morning, Jakey boy. Sleep well?"

Jake merely grunted in response. He finished buttoning his shirt and headed for the exit.

"Wait a second now. Where are you off to?"

"Work."

Clarence slipped his watch over his wrist and made a show of checking the time. "I hope some of that work includes getting Mr. Burke his money. You're already down a day. Time's ticking."

Jake clenched his jaw. He was fully aware of the deadline he was up against without Clarence's snide reminders. But pointing that out wasn't likely to make a difference, so he just opened the door and stepped outside into the gray light of pre-dawn.

The sooner he could get enough money together to get Burke off his back, the sooner Clarence would be out of his hair. His first step was to contact the owners and managers of other shows to see what he could sell, and for that, he needed Bruno.

He found the dwarf a few minutes later outside one of the bunk cars and raised a hand to him in greeting. Bruno finished running a comb through his neatly-trimmed beard and nodded to Jake. "Beautiful day for a show."

"It is," he agreed. "You busy? I could use your help with something."

"I was just getting ready for the march, but we've got a while before that starts. What can I do for you?"

"I need to get in touch with some people."

"Of course," he responded eagerly. Magical ability was rare among dwarves, and dwarf Enchanters were almost unheard of. Bruno had always been proud of the unique power that ran through his veins, and as in everything else he did, he loved any opportunity to show off his skills. "I assume you have everything we need?"

"I do."

"Lead the way, then."

They returned to Jake's sleeper car and found Clarence obstructing the doorway on his way out. Bruno scowled up at him, but the ogre didn't seem to notice.

"I was just about to go looking for you," he said. "Lucky we bumped into each other."

"Why don't you go help the men unload the tents?" Jake suggested. "I'm sure they'd appreciate the extra muscle."

Clarence's smile sagged. "I thought the two of us might be able to spend some time catching up today." Despite his crestfallen expression, his eyes were hard and cold, a clear indication that he wasn't about to let Jake get away with any nonsense.

"I'm sorry, but I've still got work to do, and I can't do it with you hovering over my shoulder every second. I'll be right here if you need me."

Clarence considered this for a few seconds. "All right then. I guess I'll see you later." His steely gaze threatened dozens of unpleasant things that would happen if for some reason they *didn't* see each other later. He stalked off, and Jake made a mental note to have a chat with him about boundaries and the importance of maintaining certain appearances. For everyone's sake.

Once they were inside with the door closed behind them, Bruno shook his head. "I don't understand how you ended up being friends with that brute."

Jake pulled a wooden crate out from under his bed and began to paw through some of his father's old belongings. "He's not so bad."

"How long did you say he was staying?"

"A few weeks." Hopefully it wouldn't be any longer than that.

Bruno sighed and muttered something under his breath. "All right then. What's this other business about?"

"I need to contact a few people on some other shows." He pulled a photo album and a handheld mirror out of the crate and brought them to Bruno.

"Perfect. Who's first?"

Jake set the photo album down and drummed his fingers against its cover. How was he going to explain this? He couldn't hide everything from his friend, but he didn't want to involve him any more than he had to. Bruno was trustworthy, but he had a tendency to overreact to bad news, and Jake was having enough trouble keeping a level head himself.

"Look," he said, "you're gonna hear some things—things I can't fully explain or justify. I know it goes without saying, but I'd appreciate it if you didn't repeat this stuff to anyone."

Bruno looked horrified at the very idea. "Jacob Strickland, I'm appalled that you would even suggest such a thing. I'm a professional. More importantly, I'm your friend. You can trust me, you know that."

"I know. But it's extra important this time."

"You have my word," he said solemnly. Who are we contacting first?"

Jake opened the photo album and turned a few pages until he found the woman he was looking for. He put a finger on her face in a newspaper photo that had been clipped nearly a decade earlier. Alexandra Armstrong owned and ran the Armstrong Family Circus with her brother, Oliver, who stood next to her in the photo. Both were fair-haired and statuesque, but where Alexandra's mouth was open and smiling, Oliver's was pinched shut and downturned. He was easily the more serious and practical of the two siblings and would thus be less inclined to make any major purchases in the middle of the season. Alexandra would be the easier sell.

Bruno studied the photograph for a few seconds, then picked up the mirror and held it so it was facing Jake. The dwarf touched the tips of his fingers to the mirror's surface. When he pulled his hand away, the reflection seemed to ripple like water, then changed so that Jake was no longer staring at his own face. Instead, the mirror showed a train yard full of men and women unloading animals and circus equipment. The scene wasn't all that different from the one currently taking place outside, but these weren't the Strickland show's train cars, and he didn't recognize any of these people. Except for one.

Alexandra Armstrong strode among her workers with her head held high and the fabric of her dress fluttering in the wind. The mirror's reflection followed her as she went, occasionally skipping to a new angle as she got father from one pane of glass and closer to another. If Jake had to guess, they were seeing her from the windows on a nearby passenger train. The enchantment would be reflecting Jake's face to her from whatever glass surface she was closest to, but to everyone else at her location, he was invisible. He doubted she was close enough to hear him, but he waved his hands in front of him, hoping the movement would catch her attention.

After a few seconds, she turned and did a double take as she caught sight of his face in one of the windows. She held up a finger to him and made her way back through the flurry of activity to a nearby boxcar. The mirror's reflection suddenly shifted so that Jake was staring at the interior of the boxcar as she entered. Racks of costumes lined the walls behind her, along with several closed trunks and instrument cases.

She stepped up to what he assumed was a dressing room mirror and touched its surface to speak with him. "Well, if it isn't Jake Strickland. My advance man says your crew put on quite the show here in Southdale last month. Townies are still talking about it. Topping that isn't going to be easy."

"I imagine you'll find a way," Jake said.

"We'll certainly try. What can I do for you?"

"I've got a business proposition for you."

"Is that so? What sort of proposition?"

"Well, to be frank, I'm afraid we've hit some hard times lately. Financial troubles."

She tilted her head. "Oh? I thought you'd already taken care of all your father's...miscalculations"

Behind the mirror, Bruno's eyes widened in curiosity. Jake chose his next words carefully. "Yes ma'am, but something else has come up. It's nothing too serious, but I don't want it to turn into a mess we can't dig ourselves out of. Point is, I've decided to downsize. I'm selling some of the animals and equipment, and I thought you and your brother might be interested."

Alexandra's eyes lit up. "That depends. What exactly are you selling?"

"A basilisk, a djinn, a chimera, two unicorns, a few phoenixes, some of the elephants and camels. Wagons, carriages, baggage stock. Anything else you're interested in, make me an offer and we can discuss it."

Her lips scrunched over to one side as she deliberated. "I don't know. It's the middle of the season. We already have our show planned out, and arranging to pick up our purchases would be a considerable inconvenience."

This had been his exact concern about attempting to sell off parts of the show in the first place, and he tried not to let his disappointment show. But circus owners were opportunists. If he could present this as a one-time chance for the Armstrong Family Circus to acquire something special and increase their profits, maybe he could convince her.

"I know you don't have a basilisk," he said.

"We had one a few years ago, but the townies didn't seem to care too much."

He feigned surprise. "Really? They're lining up in the menagerie every night to see ours. If you don't want it, I guess I can ask the Bailey brothers. Just thought I'd give you first choice. Your family was always fair in their dealings with my father, and I know he wasn't the easiest man to work with."

A muscle in Alexandra's face twitched at the mention of the Bailey brothers, her family's biggest competitors. It was a cheap trick, maybe, attempting to manipulate her with a rivalry that stretched back nearly two decades. But these were dire times.

She finally sighed and gave him a shrug. "I guess it wouldn't hurt to talk to Oliver."

His stomach sank. There was no way that penny-pincher would agree to buying anything he had to offer, but he forced a smile anyway. "You do that. And be sure to let me know what he says."

"I will. But could you do me a favor and hold off on going to the Baileys until I contact you again?"

"I'm on a pretty tight deadline here. I can't make any promises."

"A week," she pleaded. "That's all I'm asking."

"One week, then."

"Thanks. Say, what about that dragon of yours? Any chance you'd be willing to part with her?"

Jake chuckled. "I ain't *that* desperate." Or maybe he was, and he was just too stubborn to admit it yet.

"Be sure to let us know if that changes."

"Good talking to you, Alexandra. Tell your brother I said hello."

"I will. I'll talk to you again soon."

Bruno touched his fingertips to the mirror, and Jake found himself staring at his own reflection once more. "Downsizing?" the dwarf said. "I thought we were past that."

Jake flipped through the photo album in search of the next person he wanted to contact. "I thought so, too. Like I said, something else came up."

"Something I should be worried about?"

Still looking for the picture, he responded absently. "No, of course not."

"What about the other performers? The roustabouts?"

Instead of answering, Jake pointed to a man with a thin mustache in a more recent newspaper photo. "This is who we need to contact next."

"I said, is this anything we should all be concerned about?"

Something in his conscience squirmed. Payday was a little less than three weeks off, and unless he discovered a pile of forgotten gold in one of the train cars, he'd have no choice but to hold everyone's wages. Whatever it took to scrape together some of what he owed the mob.

But he couldn't tell Bruno that. There was no telling what kind of trouble he might get himself into if he knew the truth. Besides, this was Jake's problem, and he was taking care of it the best way he knew how.

So he did the only thing he could think of to do. He looked straight into his friend's eyes and told a blatant lie. "There's nothing to worry about. I promise."

Bruno studied his face for a moment, then nodded. "Okay, then. Who's next?"

Jake tapped the face of the mustached man in the photo. "Him."

"John Bailey? But you just told Miss Armstrong you'd wait to contact them."

"I know what I said. But I can't afford to wait a week just for Oliver to turn me down anyway."

Bruno was silent, but his scowl spoke volumes.

Jake was familiar with the expression. They weren't going to get anywhere until Bruno said whatever it was he thought he needed to say. "Go on, then. What is it?"

"I just don't think it's a good idea to be making enemies of other people in this business. Especially not if you're going to be calling on them for a favor in the future."

"I ain't making enemies. I'm just trying to look out for my own."

"You said there was nothing to worry about."

"There ain't."

Bruno cocked his head to one side. "But the situation is bad enough that you need to lie to get this money together?"

"It ain't a lie, exactly. It's just—"

"Sneaky," Bruno finished for him. "It's sneaky. And you're not a sneaky man, Jake. You have more integrity than that."

Jake sighed. No one in his entire life had ever been quite as good at putting him through a guilt trip as Bruno. Not Ma, not even Grace. "All right. I won't offer them the basilisk, then. But they're a big show, and if anyone has money to spare, it's them. I have to at least reach out. Maybe that makes me sneaky, but I can't worry about that now."

Bruno's frown deepened. "What is it that has you so scared?"

Jake averted his eyes and tapped John Bailey's face in the photo again. "Come on. Let's just get this over with."

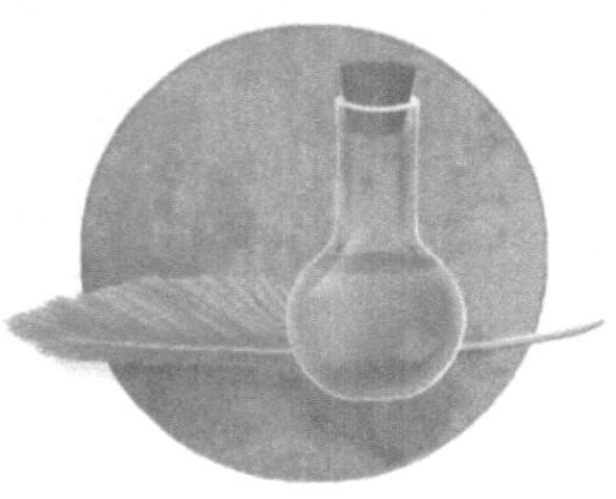

# CHAPTER 6

## HEY RUBE

Two days later, all Jake had managed to sell was a chimera, a djinn, and a pair of camels. John Bailey had offered him a fair price for the chimera, but the money he got for the djinn and the camels was barely enough to be worth the effort. If things continued at this rate, he wouldn't have Burke's money until well past the deadline, assuming he was even still alive by then.

He contacted a few more people with Bruno's mirror enchantments before the two of them made their way to the cookhouse for a late breakfast. Jake didn't have much of an appetite and gave up halfway through the meal. He left Bruno sitting alone and headed to the ticket booth instead, partly out of a sense of self-imposed duty to welcome the townies to his circus, but mostly because he wanted to count them. Ticket sales alone weren't going to save his show, but if he got enough of them every day from now until Burke's deadline, they could put a sizeable dent in his debt.

Or at least, that was what he wanted to believe.

His curiosity piqued as he drew closer to the booth. An extra line had formed off to one side, and several of the townies were filtering directly into this new queue after purchasing their general admission tickets. Otto's ten-year-old twins, Thelma and Alice, sat behind a folding card table taking the townies' money and handing back change. On occasion, the circus kids would set up a lemonade stand next to the grease joint to make a little money off thirsty passersby, but this was something different. What were they up to?

Alice stamped the tickets of a family of five and returned them with a cheerful wave. "Have fun!"

"Be sure to tell your friends," Thelma said as she passed a few bills back to a young couple.

Jake walked past them. He peered through the mass of legs and bodies in line and caught a glimpse of a hand-painted sign taped to the front of the table. *Brush the griffins! Bathe the dragon!* Prices were listed below each item—almost double the cost of what the circus charged for general admission.

He cringed inwardly as he imagined all the ways this business venture could go wrong, but he kept a calm demeanor as he approached the table and crouched down next to Thelma behind it. "Hey, girls," he said, tipping his hat to them.

"Hi, Mr. Strickland," Thelma replied. Alice was busy talking to a customer but flashed him a quick grin.

"What are you two up to here?"

"We're helping Ms. Hawkins," Thelma said, taking a crisp five-dollar bill from a customer and counting out his change. "She said we could keep some of the money if we stamp people's tickets."

"Grace put you up to this?"

Thelma nodded.

"Where is she now?"

"Over by the menagerie with our dad."

"And they're just...letting people give Calico Thunder a bath?"

Thelma nodded again. "And brush Trigger and Bullseye. It's a big hit. If we keep doing this, me and Alice will definitely have enough money to buy our own bicycles by the end of summer. We're going to start our own act, you know. Mr. Laurent says he'll teach us how to ride on the tightrope."

Jake smiled. Thelma and Alice would be lucky if their father even considered allowing them to do such a stunt. Otto was far more protective of his girls than most of the other circus parents. Ironic, considering the man spent his days looking after some of the world's most dangerous creatures.

"Keep up the good work." He tipped his hat to them, then stood and went to look for Grace.

He found her behind the menagerie tent. Or rather, he found a gathering of about a hundred townies clustered together around some spectacle. He skirted the edge of the crowd and eventually reached the outer perimeter of a portable corral typically used to let the horses and unicorns graze. Now, however, it was being used as a grooming station for Trigger, Bullseye, and Calico Thunder.

Otto and three of his workmen stood to one side of the corral with the griffins. They passed brushes between the townies on the other side of the fence, who seemed delighted by the opportunity to get so close to some of the circus' most majestic creatures. The griffins' sharp beaks were muzzled, leaving just enough space between the wires to let them snap up the tiny bites of meat Otto offered as a reward for their patience.

Jake watched their behavior closely, looking for signs of irritation or annoyance. The griffins were generally friendly and well-behaved, having been raised by humans since birth. But they were still wild animals, and even if their beaks were muzzled, one slash from their powerful talons could do mutilating damage.

But they didn't look irritated. If anything, they seemed to enjoy all the extra attention. Bullseye was leaning into his brushing, eyes half-closed in contentment, and Trigger happily gulped down a piece of meat before prancing obediently to the next section of fence, where a woman waited to run a wide-toothed comb through his chest feathers.

Maybe this wasn't such a terrible idea after all. At least, not where the griffins were concerned. Calico Thunder might be a different story.

He turned his attention to the other side of the corral, where Grace stood next to the dragon on a patch of wet grass. Calico Thunder lazed on the ground with her neck and tail fully extended, soaking up the rays of the warm sun overhead. A large tub of soapy water sat near her snout, and Grace offered a wide push broom to a townie outside the corral. The man leaned over the fence to dip the bristles in the water. Then, under Grace's direction, he began to scrub the dragon's scales.

She opened her one good eye when the broom touched her shoulder, but shut it again after a few seconds and allowed the man to scrub without complaint. Like the griffins, her mouth was muzzled, and her wings were bound in their usual fashion to keep her from flying off. The chain around her right foreleg would prevent her from getting too close to the townies should she decide to get up. But with Grace at her side, talking to her in soft, encouraging murmurs, she seemed content to lie in the sun with soapy water rolling down her scales.

Jake hopped over the fence and stomped his feet as he approached, a courtesy to Calico Thunder to make sure he didn't startle her. She opened her eye and fixed her gaze on him for a few seconds, then snorted and rolled over to sun her left side. A group of kids straddling the fence giggled to each other as they watched her.

"Hey, cowboy," Grace greeted him. She didn't take her eyes off the townie holding the broom.

Jake gave her hand a quick squeeze. "Thelma and Alice told me about your little side business here. I thought I'd come check it out."

"Thought you'd come tell me what a bad idea this is, you mean," she teased.

"I admit that may have crossed my mind. I should have known you'd have everything under control."

She went to take the broom from the man. After rinsing the bristles in the tub, she passed it to the next person, pocketing his ticket as she returned to Jake's side. "Are you admitting you were wrong, then?"

He chuckled. "All right, then. I was wrong. Wouldn't be the first time."

"I was going to run it past you before I started, but you've been so busy with Bruno, and Calico Thunder needed a good scrubbing anyway."

"It's smart. Where'd you come up with the idea?"

"It's been floating around my head for a while now. I never got around to actually making it happen, but I figured now's as good a time as any. I want to do my part. It's not much, but the extra money could help. Right?"

Guilt snaked its way up through Jake's chest. This wasn't just some innovative new idea to engage their audience. This was about the money he owed Burke.

When he'd confided in her and asked for her advice on how to resolve the issue, he hadn't expected her to take his troubles upon herself. All he'd wanted was someone to talk to and bounce ideas off of. This was *his* problem, not hers. A part of him was touched by her concern and her willingness to help—grateful, even. But he hadn't meant for her to take on personal responsibility like this.

But of course she had, because that was what Grace did. She was always looking out for other people, always doing whatever she could to help her circus family. He should have thought of that before he told her anything.

She nudged him out of his ruminating with an elbow in the side. "What's with the long face?"

"Just thinking."

"Well, whatever unhappy thoughts you've got churning around in there, stop it. We're going to be okay. We'll figure this out. Together."

"Grace, I don't expect you to get involved in this. I can take care of it on my own. It ain't your problem."

She took his hand. "Of course it is. I love you. Your problems are my problems. We're a team, aren't we?"

He sighed. "We are, but—"

"But nothing."

She passed the scrub broom to the next waiting townie and directed him to wash Calico Thunder's haunches. When she returned to Jake's side, she linked her arm through his and leaned against his shoulder. "You know, one of these days, you're going to have to learn to take help when you need it. Until then, I'll be here to give it to you whether you ask for it or not."

He kissed the top of her head. "Thanks. I—"

A griffin's screech and an angry shout from the other side of the corral cut him off. He turned around just in time to see a surly-faced townie punch one of Otto's workmen in the jaw. Bullseye reared up on his back legs and started to unfurl his wings.

Grace gasped. "Oh no!"

"Stay here." Jake took off at a dead sprint toward the griffins. Otto and one of the workmen quickly got Bullseye under control, but the roustabout who'd been attacked was now attempting to climb over the fence to get to his assailant.

The townie backed away with a smug expression. As if to taunt the circus worker, he waved something in front of him. A few more steps brought Jake close enough to see what it was—a feather from one of the griffins.

Of course it was. He'd been a fool not to see that coming.

Otto led the griffins away from the fence. Shouts from the crowd were making them restless, but not unduly so. Not yet. Jake took their lead ropes from Otto and pointed to the townie who had instigated the fight. "Get him out of here. And get your man under control."

Otto rushed to the fence. After a brief scuffle, he and the other two workmen managed to pull down their enraged companion.

“That’s enough, Walt!” Otto shouted. “Let him go.”

Walt yanked free of Otto’s grasp and tugged on his clothes to straighten them out. He cast a dark look at the townie behind the fence and flung his arm out as if to shoo the man away. “Get him the hell away from me, then.”

“Go on boys,” Otto said to the other workmen. “You heard the boss. Get him out of here.”

They hopped the fence and stalked toward the man like a pair of angry bulldogs. He managed to tuck the griffin feather safely inside his shirt before they grabbed him roughly by both arms and spun him around. As they led him though the crowd back to the ticket booth, the townies booed. A few even threw things at him.

At least they weren’t taking his side. Larger fights between townies and circus folk could get ugly fast—Jake knew that from personal experience.

Otto shook his head and moved closer to Jake. Walt stood by sullenly and rubbed at the bottom of his jaw.

“It wasn’t the boy’s fault,” Otto said. “That damn rube just—”

“Not now,” Jake said flatly. “Come find me at showtime. We can talk about it then.”

“Sure, boss.”

Jake handed back the griffins’ lead ropes. Putting on his most gentlemanly smile, he stepped forward to address the townies. “Well folks, that got pretty exciting for a minute, didn’t it?”

A few of them chuckled. More smiled, reflecting Jake’s own air of cheerful nonchalance. He may not have had Bruno’s showmanship skills, but he’d quickly learned how to step in and put people at ease when something in the circus went wrong. The trick was to act like everything was going exactly according to plan, even in the midst of chaos.

“Unfortunately, I think that was a little *too* much excitement for Trigger and Bullseye here. We’ll need to give them a break so they can perform their best later this afternoon. I'm gonna have to ask you all to go back to the ticket line and get a refund." He looked over his shoulder to where Calico Thunder was still stretched out lazily in the sun. A little boy was scrubbing her behind the horns with his mother's help. "Or, if you'd rather, you can use your griffin-brushing tickets to give Calico Thunder over there a good bath. She still seems to be enjoying herself."

Some of the townies laughed again. Several made a beeline for the other side of the corral while others meandered off toward the ticket booth for a refund. With only a few stragglers remaining, Jake turned to Otto and Walt. "You two go talk to the gals at the ticket booth. Let them know what happened, then go find some patches to help smooth this over."

"I'm real sorry, Mr. Strickland," Walt said, twisting a handkerchief in his hands. "I wasn't trying to start any trouble, I just—"

"Hush. You just go on and make things right, you hear?"

"Yes, sir."

"Otto, we'll talk later?"

The man nodded and handed the griffins' ropes back to Jake, then headed off with Walt to complete their assigned tasks.

Jake led Trigger and Bullseye out of the corral and back to the ring stock tent. As they walked, Bullseye extended his wings and fanned them a few times to cool himself. There was a noticeable gap in his secondary feathers along the edge of his left wing, roughly the same length and width as the feather that townie had been waving around.

Jake clenched his jaw. Picking up a fallen feather from the ground was one thing, but plucking it off the creature was inexcusable. If that was what had happened, Walt had had every right to react the way he did. And if that wasn't what had happened...well, it was only a matter of time before it *did*.

He gave Bullseye a pat on the side and ushered him into his stall behind his brother. A shame he'd have to shut this attraction down before it had really even gotten started.

They might still be able to get away with letting the townies bathe Calico Thunder, but allowing them to brush the griffins was out of the question.

Grace was going to be disappointed. It had been such a good idea, and if she'd started this up a few years ago—before the Ban—there probably wouldn't have been any trouble. As it was now, they had to put the safety of the animals first. She of all people would understand that.

# CHAPTER 7

## ILLUSIONS

Later that night, Grace stood beside Jake on the sidelines of the circus floor. He watched the flicker of orange flames dancing in her eyes, a reflection from the eight fiery torches flying through the air in the center ring. A pair of jugglers tossed them up and caught them again in a series of practiced movements almost too fast for the eye to follow. The audience looked on in mesmerized silence while the band played a suspenseful tune to evoke a sense of excitement and danger.

"I should have known something like that would happen," Grace said, shaking her head. "You're right, of course. We'll have to shut it down."

"At least with the griffins," Jake replied. "As long as the townies stay outside the fence, I don't see the harm in letting them scrub Calico Thunder."

"I'm sorry."

"What for? It was a good idea. It ain't your fault we can't trust half the folks who come through here."

"I know. I just really wanted to do something useful. You've been working so hard trying to get that money for Burke, and I just...I hate feeling so helpless."

Jake put an arm around her shoulders. "Grace Hawkins,

you are the least helpless woman I know. Besides, wasn't it you who told me we're gonna figure this out?"

She smiled back at him. "I know we will."

The music stopped. The jugglers extinguished their torches in two buckets of water and took their bows in front of the cheering crowd.

"I'd better go get the animals ready," Grace said, stepping out from beneath Jake's arm. He gave her a quick kiss and watched her follow the jugglers out of the big top.

Illuminated by a single spotlight, Bruno stepped into the ring to announce the next act. "And now, ladies and gentlemen, please welcome to the center ring one of the world's most talented illusionists. I present to you the incredible, the magnificent, the incomparable Madame Arabella!"

The spotlight shifted from Bruno to Madame Arabella. She sashayed to the center in a lavish black gown, her short, raven hair framing her face. Unlike the rest of the performers, she did not to engage with the audience in any sort of amicable way. Instead, she looked out at the crowd with haughty disdain, as if they and the circus itself were beneath her.

A nagging sense of annoyance rose up inside of Jake, and he tried to recall the amount of time remaining on the illusionist's contract. Seven—no, closer to eight months. It might as well have been an eternity.

If he did end up having to hold the performers' pay, maybe she'd quit on her own. A man could dream.

Madame Arabella stood motionless until the audience quieted. Only when the entire big top was dead silent did she begin her act. She raised her hands, and a lone clarinet began a melodic tune in a gentle, lilting voice.

A figure rose up from the ground to Madame Arabella's side, a woman made of light and magic. Jake recognized her instantly as Princess Callista and was familiar with the story Madame Arabella was about to weave. It was an old folk tale Ma used to tell him. Though the illusionist always put her own spin on it, the basic structure of the story was the same, following the princess on her quest to save her kingdom from a terrible curse.

Callista began to dance, far more lithe and graceful than any corporeal being could ever hope to be. Flowers and trees sprang up wherever she walked, and a gently flowing stream cut its way through the center of the big top. Butterflies and fairies darted through the air, and squirrels chased each other up the trees. The sounds of birds singing and water flowing soon mingled with the clarinet's song, and Jake swore he could feel a cool spring breeze blowing across his skin. There was even a castle up on a hill in the distance, the shining beacon of Callista's kingdom.

Regardless of his personal distaste for Madame Arabella, Jake couldn't deny her skill. Bruno hadn't exaggerated when he'd announced her as one of the most talented illusionists in the world.

A voice to his left broke his immersion in the magical display. "Hey boss," Otto said. "You wanted to talk to me?"

Jake turned to the man. "You wanna tell me exactly what happened at the corral earlier?"

Otto scratched at the scruff under his jaw. "I didn't see the first bit, but Walt says that townie just grabbed one of Bullseye's feathers and yanked it right off. Walt told him he couldn't do that, tried to take the feather back from the man, and...well, things got a little out of hand."

"Over a feather," Jake said flatly.

Otto shoved his hands in his pockets and stared at his feet. "I'm afraid that's right, boss."

Jake turned back to Madame Arabella's illusion. The curse had come upon Princess Callista's kingdom, and all the vibrant trees and flowers shriveled up right before the audience's eyes as an eerie red light filled the big top. Twisting shadows slithered in from the canvas sidewalls, overtaking the peaceful beauty that had been present just moments ago. A cacophony of drums and low brass drowned out the clarinet's melody as the rest of the band took up a far more ominous tune.

"I can't have your crew attacking the customers."

Otto shook his head. "It won't happen again."

"I hope not. Look, up until now, I ain't said a word about all the discarded feathers and scales and hairs your men collect. As long as they do their job and no harm comes to the animals, there's no problem. They wanna take a risk and try to make a profit from this Ban, that's their choice. I don't wanna be involved. But when fights break out between your men and the townies, I have to get involved. You understand?"

"I understand."

"All it takes is one over-enthusiastic, off-duty cop to see that sort of thing and decide to do a full investigation. That causes delays, and it could mean they shut us down. We don't need any setbacks. Especially not now."

"Especially not now?" The pitch of Otto's voice raised a little higher than usual at the end of the question.

"What?"

"Well, it's just that...there have been rumors, you know."

"What kinds of rumors?"

"About the show. How you're trying to sell off parts of it."

Jake inhaled deeply, catching a whiff of salty ocean air as a cold spray misted against his skin. In the center ring, enormous waves swelled on a stormy sea, and a flash of lightning illuminated Princess Callista's boat. It bucked and spun in the violent storm, completely out of her control. She threw herself onto the deck and clasped her hands together in a desperate prayer. But with the next flash of lightning, an angry wave slammed against her small craft, plunging both it and her into the dark depths below.

The music stopped, and for a few seconds, all seemed lost. The audience leaned forward. Jake held his breath with them.

There was a low drumroll from the band, then a sudden burst of song as a sleek sea dragon broke through the water. On his back rode Princess Callista, proud and triumphant, her long hair streaming out behind her like a banner. She clung to the dragon's scales as it carried her through the storm and across the sea to a verdant tropical island.

Was riding a sea dragon anything like riding a dragon through the air? It had been such a long time since Jake had experienced the thrill, he was starting to forget what it felt like.

"Boss?"

He blinked and turned back to Otto. What had they just been talking about? Oh, right—rumors. "It's just business. Nothing to worry about."

"Oh, of course not. I didn't mean to imply...well, never mind." He crossed his arms and rocked back on his heels.

They watched the climax of Madame Arabella's performance together in silence. The sea dragon bore Princess Callista back across the waves to her cursed kingdom, and a grand battle ensued as she fought off the darkness with a flaming sword and her own magic.

Otto jerked a nod over his shoulder. "I should be getting back to the menagerie to help the boys pack up. Unless there's something else you wanted to talk to me about?"

Jake shook his head. "No, go on. Thanks for all your hard work."

The man turned and walked out of the big top as Princess Callista defeated the last of the shadows and brought life and beauty to her kingdom again. The illusion began to fade, and soon, Madame Arabella stood alone in the center ring once more.

Pride warmed inside Jake's chest with the cheers and applause that erupted to fill the big top. It wasn't his performance, but he liked to believe his role in bringing the show together was an important one.

During moments like this, he could understand his father's passion for the magic and grandeur of the circus—how it could become so intoxicating that it turned into an obsession. He sympathized with Cliff a little more in moments like this. Not for long, but enough to make him wonder if he'd always been a little too hard on the man.

Something brushed against his arm, and he turned to see Clarence's massive figure standing next to him. His joy and pride shattered inside him in an instant.

The ogre clapped as Madame Arabella exited the ring. Jake tipped his hat to her on her way out of the big top. She raised her chin higher and stared down her nose at him in return.

"What a performance that was, eh, Jakey boy?" said Clarence. "Absolutely incredible. You really do have some talented people here."

He forced out an appropriate response between clenched teeth. "Thank you."

"It really would be a shame if any of them got caught up in this *arrangement* you have with Mr. Burke. Things can get a little messy sometimes, if you know what I mean. It's unfortunate, but it happens when people stick their noses in places they don't belong." The threat dripped from his words like poison.

"I haven't told them anything."

"Really? Because your girlfriend has been giving me some awfully mean looks lately. The dwarf, too."

"That's just Bruno," Jake said, trying to sound calm. "He doesn't know anything. And Grace—I only told her because I need her help getting the money."

Clarence stared down at him and raised an eyebrow.

"I won't say a word to anyone else. Promise."

"Good. But do you really expect to get all that money together in time? The way you're going about it doesn't seem to be very effective. I hear you had a bit of trouble with one of your griffins earlier today."

Jake frowned. How much did Clarence even know about what he was doing? The ogre checked up on him at regular intervals throughout the day, but aside from that, he seemed content to let Jake go about his business without interference. Still, news traveled fast on a show like this, and maybe he'd been listening to the same rumors Otto had. Either way, Jake wasn't about to give him any additional details.

"Burke will get his money. That's all that matters."

"I hope so," Clarence said. He raised his hand and tapped the face of his watch with a thick finger. "You're already down to twenty-seven days. Tick tock."

# CHAPTER 8

## A DROP IN THE BUCKET

"It's the best we can offer. I can send some people over to pick it up in a few days if you're willing to take the deal."

Jake already knew his answer, but he made a show of considering Alexandra's offer for a few seconds before responding. He'd waited the full week she'd requested, and he could wait a few seconds more. No reason to let her see just how desperate he was.

In the mirror's reflection, Alexandra sighed and put her hands on her hips. "Oh, come on now. You wouldn't have reached out at all if you thought you had better options, and you'll be hard pressed to find any other shows willing to take on the care of a fifty-foot long snake."

"It's a little more than a *snake*. You might wanna remind your people of that when they come to pick it up."

She waved a hand dismissively. "Yes, I know. But with the enchantments containing it, it can't actually harm—wait. Does this mean you're accepting the deal?"

"I'd be a fool not to."

"Oh, good! Oliver's going to be so delighted. He's always loved reptiles. Let's see, then. Where will you be playing on the seventeenth?"

Jake thought about it for a few seconds, trying to recall their planned route for the week. Behind the mirror, Bruno mouthed the answer to him.

"Cedar Hills," he said. "We've got a two-day stand there, Tuesday and Wednesday."

"Excellent," Alexandra replied. "I'll send my men with the money. They should arrive Tuesday, if they don't run into any trouble on the way."

"I'll keep an eye out for them."

"All right, then." She sighed and glanced at something to her left, out of the mirror's view. "I should get back to work. Oh, but before I go, you haven't given any more thought to selling that dragon of yours, have you?"

Jake grinned and shook his head. "Goodbye, Alexandra."

Bruno touched his fingers to the mirror and set it down. "Well, that's good news."

Jake grunted a response as he flipped through the pages of his father's old photo album, searching the faces inside for anyone he and Bruno might have overlooked. He was nine thousand dollars closer to his goal now that he'd sold the basilisk, but nine thousand was an awfully small drop in a bucket of four hundred thousand.

"Isn't it?"

He glanced up at his friend. "What?"

Bruno cocked his head to the side. "You've been waiting on that deal for a week. I thought you'd be happier about it. It's a lot of money."

Jake forced himself to smile. "I am happy. You're right, it's a lot of money." And yet, so very, very little. As Clarence had reminded him this morning, he only had twenty-three days left to pay his debt.

Still, at least it was something.

"Maybe it's not my place," Bruno said, "but some of the others are starting to worry. I'm sure you've heard the rumors."

He had, more and more frequently of late. Rumors spread faster than wildfire among troupers, even between different shows. He and Bruno had contacted every big show in the country by now. Of course word had gotten around.

"They're just rumors," he muttered.

"Maybe so, but people are getting spooked, afraid of losing their jobs. Or not getting paid. Some say the circus is hemorrhaging money, and we're all about to lose everything."

"That's not true."

"All I'm saying is if there's any way to put their minds at ease, you might want to consider it."

Jake rubbed at his eyes. They felt dry and gritty, like someone had poured sand in them. His sleep had been fitful the last few nights. Doubts and worries ran endless circles in his mind, and even when he did manage to drift off, it wasn't for very long. Now, it was barely even morning, and already he wanted to go back to bed and shut out the rest of the world.

But that wasn't going to make any of his problems go away.

Bruno patted his arm. "Don't fret. I know it's all just fearmongering, and those of us who were here before your dad passed keep telling everyone things are going to work out. After all, you've pulled us through harder times than this. Coming in here and turning things around the way you did—we haven't forgotten."

Jake's gut twisted, and for a second, he was tempted to tell Bruno everything. But what good would it do? He'd already burdened Grace with his problem, and Clarence had made it clear he shouldn't tell any of the others. He wasn't sure what the consequences of the threat entailed, but he didn't want to find out.

"I appreciate that," he said instead. The words tasted like ash in his mouth.

Concern lingered in Bruno's eyes. "Are you sure everything's all right? You haven't been yourself lately. I know I've asked before, but is this something we should be worried about? Should I be worried about *you*?"

He started to shake his head, then stopped himself and spoke the closest thing to the truth he dared. "I don't know."

"Is there anything I can do?"

"You're already doing it. I appreciate your help with these enchantments."

"Sure, whatever you need." He patted Jake's arm again. "You'll figure it out. I have faith in you."

Jake wished he could believe that faith hadn't been misplaced.

♦ ♦ ♦

When the circus train rolled into Cedar Hills on July seventeenth, the sky was gray and overcast. They got through the march and most of the setup on the lot without so much as a drop of rain, but by the time the afternoon show began, the sky was dumping water.

Bruno cast enchantments over the tents to prevent the stakes from being loosened in the mud and to keep everything relatively dry. Maintaining the spells required his constant attention, so he wasn't able to announce the show. One of the clowns took his place, but he wasn't nearly as charismatic, and he bungled the order of several acts. Whether because of the rain or the lackluster performance or both, several townies left their seats at intermission and went to the ticket booth to demand a refund.

Jake tried not to let any of this bother him, but when Alexandra Armstrong's people failed to show up for the basilisk she'd agreed to purchase, his mood soured.

"Maybe they just got caught up in the storm," Grace said as they ate a quick supper before the evening show. "I'm sure they'll be here tomorrow."

The rain let up by morning, and Jake spent the rest of the next day watching for Alexandra's men. He stayed on the lot while the roustabouts loaded the last poles of the big top into wagons. He stayed even after they were gone, lantern in hand, listening for the sound of approaching tires or wagon wheels or voices in the dark. He stayed for another hour after that, until the train manager came to find him, red-faced and huffing, insisting that they needed to leave immediately or they weren't going to make their next stop in time.

No one came. He jogged back to the train yard, still holding onto the faintest glimmer of hope that they might be waiting for him there, but they weren't. So instead of climbing into his train car, he went to the performers' sleeper car to find Bruno.

The train started rolling to their next destination, and he motioned for Bruno to follow him. They headed for one of the baggage cars. Jake pushed his way through racks of costumes until he found the small vanity Madame Arabella insisted they pack everywhere for her exclusive personal use. The three-panel mirror standing up along the far edge would be adequate for contacting Alexandra, and this way he could have the conversation away from Clarence's eavesdropping.

Bruno shoved his way through the mass of fabrics. He looked between Jake and the mirror and cocked his head. "You want to contact someone now? It's the middle of the night."

"Alexandra Armstrong," he said. "Her men never arrived. I just wanna make sure everything's okay."

"She may not even be awake," Bruno said, but he shuffled around to the other side of the mirror and touched its surface anyway.

Moments later, Alexandra's face appeared in the reflection. She sat on the edge of her bed, reading a book by lantern light in a personal train car not unlike Jake's. It only took a few seconds for her to spot them in the reflection. Her jaw tightened as she stood up and touched her own mirror to communicate with them.

"I was wondering when I might hear from you." Icy hostility laced her voice. But why?

"Sorry for the late-night intrusion," Jake said. "I won't take up much of your time. It's just that your people never showed up to get that basilisk, and I got worried. I wanted to let you know, just in case something happened to them."

"Worried, huh?" Her expression remained flat and unconcerned. "Well, worry no more, Mr. Strickland. My people are just fine. In fact, I never sent them."

"You never..." Clearly, he was missing something. "I'm sorry, but why not?"

She shrugged dramatically. "Why not? I wonder."

He glanced at Bruno. The dwarf stared back at him with a knowing expression, but Jake still couldn't figure out what he was missing.

"I hear the Bailey brothers recently acquired a chimera," Alexandra said.

*Shit.* He'd forgotten. Or maybe he'd just shoved it way back in his mind because he hadn't wanted to deal with it. Bruno's gaze bored into him, carrying with it a very clear *I told you so.*

He ran a hand across the back of his neck. "I'm sorry, Alexandra. I shouldn't have gone to them behind your back."

She rolled her eyes. "One week. That's all I wanted, just one week."

"I told you I couldn't make any promises."

"You told me you'd wait. I didn't think you were the kind of man who needs an explicit promise to hold him to his word. I thought you were better than that—better than your father. Turns out, you're just like him. And I don't make deals with people I can't trust."

Her words burned hotter than any flame ever could. Burned because they were true, at least on some level. So instead of responding with any of the numerous denials running through his mind, he shrugged. "You ain't wrong. But I don't wanna be like him. It was a mistake, and I really am sorry. Let me make it right."

For a moment, her expression softened, and it looked like she might be willing to forgive him. Then she sighed and shook her head. "It's too late for that."

"Please."

She reached toward the mirror. "I'm sorry. The deal's off. Goodnight."

"Wait—"

She was already gone.

Bruno stepped around the vanity and headed for the door to return to his sleeper car. Jake watched him go, waiting for him to say something, to remind Jake he'd been right all along. But he reached for the door, and the words never came.

If he wasn't going to say anything, Jake would do it for him. "You were right." he said. "Don't you wanna stick around and rub that in a little?" He tried to infuse a little humor into his voice, but it just came out black and twisted.

Bruno turned and gave him a sad smile. "It seems like you're doing a pretty good job of beating yourself up already. And you've told me all you're going to tell me, so I'm not really sure what else there is for me to say." He sighed and held his arms out at his sides. "I don't know how to help you, Jake."

The train went around a particularly hard turn, and they both had to brace themselves against the wall to keep from stumbling.

Jake straightened. "I'm sorry." He had so many things to apologize for. For getting Bruno involved in his problems, for keeping secrets, for behaving in ways that must seem confusing and uncharacteristic from the outside. For telling lies and half-truths while Bruno did all he could to defend Jake and reassure the others that what was happening wouldn't impact them.

But most of all, he needed to apologize because for the first time since this had all begun, he could see no way out, and that meant when Burke's deadline came, Bruno and everyone else on this show would be affected. Without the circus, they'd lose their jobs, their home, and their community in a single sweep. It seemed as inevitable as death.

"Get some sleep," Bruno said. "Who knows? Maybe things will look a little brighter in the morning."

He exited the car, leaving Jake alone in the dark with only his own dread and regret to keep him company.

# CHAPTER 9

## JUST YOU, JUST ME

Nobody else wanted the basilisk.

Jake contacted every show he and Bruno could think of over the next three days, but he had no luck selling much of anything. And the more time passed, the more disheartened he grew.

With just sixteen days left until Burke came for his money, he sat under the shade of the cookhouse and picked at his breakfast in silence. Grace kept glancing up at him over the table. She was worried. Not just about the debt, but about him. She'd told him as much several times and had even talked him into taking a mild sleeping potion she'd brewed up. It helped a little, but despite all his reassurances that she needn't worry, she continued to keep a close eye on him.

The table they were sitting at slowly cleared as people finished their meals and left one by one. Once Bruno was gone, Grace leaned over the table to speak to Jake in a hushed, secretive tone. "Did you get any offers this morning?"

He shook his head. "No."

A frown flitted at the corners of her mouth. Just for a moment, but it was enough for him to see her disappointment. She quickly masked it with a smile. "Well, we've still got some time."

"Not much. My luck had better change fast, or I ain't gonna—"

"Yes!" She straightened up so fast she nearly jumped off the bench, and her eyes suddenly brightened. "That's genius. That's exactly what you need. Why didn't I think of that before?"

"What?"

"*Luck*. That's what this is—bad luck." She leaned in toward him and lowered her voice to a near whisper. "You need a luck charm."

He considered the idea for a few seconds. A luck charm *would* be helpful, and maybe it was time to accept the fact that more drastic measures were needed if he wanted to meet Burke's deadline. The tiniest spark of hope flickered to life inside his chest.

There was just one minor complication. "Charms are illegal."

Grace rolled her eyes. "You're such a goody two-shoes sometimes. This is a matter of life and death. Who cares if you have to break a few rules to survive?"

"But the Ban—"

"The Ban is for prudes and anti-magic zealots. Look, it's perfect. We've got a two-day stand here, and there must be at least a dozen joints in town selling charms and jinxes on the sly. All we need to do is find one. We go there tonight, buy what we need, and walk out. Easy."

As far as rules went, the Ban *was* a little ridiculous—on that much, they could both agree. After all, what gave a handful of people in power the right to vilify a unique form of magic and prohibit anyone from ever using it? The only thing that separated charms and jinxes from other types of magic was that they had a long history of being used to harm others or give a person an unfair advantage in certain ventures. An almost arbitrary distinction, since other magical practices could technically be used to do the exact same thing, albeit a little less directly. But whether he liked it or not, the Ban was law, and he couldn't take that lightly. Going to some underground speakeasy to illegally purchase forbidden magic wasn't an idea he normally would have even entertained.

At this point, though, did he really have any better options? He looked over his shoulder and caught Clarence staring at him. As the ogre kept reminding him, the clock was ticking. Fast.

"All right," he said. "Let's do it. Where do you suppose we find one of these joints?"

"I'll take care of that part. Meet me in the menagerie after the evening show. Just make sure you ditch your guard." She put a hand on his arm and gave him a flirtatious smile. "And wear something nice. If we're going to do this, we might as well have a little fun with it."

♦ ♦ ♦

Ditching Clarence proved to be more difficult than Jake had anticipated, and it was well after dark by the time he was able to meet Grace in the menagerie. Most days, the tent would have been one of the first things to be torn down and packed up as townies moved into the big top for the evening's final performance, but whenever they stayed somewhere overnight, it remained standing. The place always looked a little eerie in the dark, with strange sounds and shadows that weren't always identifiable. Something shifted in the shadows and hissed as he approached, and he quickened his pace to hurry past.

He found Grace in front of the fairy box, watching the flickering glow of the tiny creatures inside their large glass tank. They were much livelier at night, and Jake had often thought it a shame that the townies only ever got to see them during the day when they were sleeping. Now, they chased each other through the wildflowers and toadstools like rainbow-colored fireflies, each one no bigger than his thumb.

Grace turned at his approach. A simple white dress fell just above her knees, and she'd pulled her long hair up in the back. A few loose waves fell free around her face, which had been dusted with makeup to enhance the delicate contours of her cheekbones. Her warm eyes smiled at him from beneath long, dark lashes.

She looked stunning. She always looked beautiful to him, but even dressed in the best shirt and slacks he owned, he felt like a peasant standing in front of an angel.

She looked him up and down and nodded approvingly. "You look good."

"I could say the same to you."

"Why, thank you." She made a little curtsy. "It took you long enough to get here."

"Sorry. I had a hard time getting away from Clarence."

Grace winked at him over her shoulder as she turned to head for the exit. "So he enjoys your company. Are you really going to fault him for that?"

Jake stroked the stubble on his chin and cocked his head to one side. "Hmm. You might be right. I've been told I have a very magnetic personality."

She laughed. "And so humble, too. The complete package. What a lucky girl I am, to have a man like you."

"You really are." He pretended to stumble as she gave him a playful jab in the arm.

It wasn't true. *He* was the lucky one, not her. Luck charm or not, with her by his side, he would always consider himself a fortunate man.

He pushed aside the menagerie's canvas flap and held it open for her, then offered her his arm once they were outside. She took it, and they matched each other's steps on their way to the road. Lanterns still lit several of the smaller tents they passed. Inside, troupers gathered together to drink, laugh, tell stories, and play cards. Jake loved the atmosphere of the circus on nights like this. Not having to tear everything down and hurry away to their next destination meant they could relax and enjoy some rare downtime before the next day's show.

Considering what he'd likely have to tell them about their wages in the next few days, it was possibly the last carefree night they were going to have for a while.

He tried to push those thoughts out of his mind, at least for now. The summer air was pleasantly cool and fresh, and here on the outskirts of town, the sky overhead was soaked in starlight. He was with Grace, and they were happy, and they were on an adventure together. Aside from the events which had prompted that adventure, it was the perfect night.

They made their way into the city and walked through unfamiliar streets, occasionally passing fellow strangers in the night. Grace stopped periodically to check their location on a map in her beaded clutch. Eventually, they found themselves in front of a back-alley door somewhere near the center of town. She knocked a rhythmic pattern on its surface. A narrow, rectangular panel at the top slid open, and the man behind it peered out at them with narrowed eyes. "Yes?"

"We're here for Raymond's show," Grace said.

The panel slid shut, and there was a click and a jangle as the man turned a deadbolt and removed a chain before swinging the door open. He looked them over for a few seconds, then ushered them inside.

The establishment was small and cozy, with tables and chairs lining the walls on three sides and a bar in one corner. Glass bottles of all shapes and sizes lined the shelves behind the counter, the larger ones filled with alcohol and the smaller containing a colorful variety of less identifiable substances in solid, liquid, and vaporous forms. A jazz band played on a raised platform in another corner, and couples packed the dance floor in the center of the room, skipping and spinning in time with the lively music.

Jake turned to Grace. Her cheeks were flushed, and her eyes seemed to sparkle brighter than usual. She grabbed his hand and led him through the throng of dancing couples to a vacant table on the other side of the room. It was small and round, barely larger than either of the two stools that stood beside it. When they sat down, they were so close their knees brushed against each other, but Jake didn't mind.

He looked around the crowded room, and his eyes fell on a familiar face at the bar. It was Walt, the same roustabout who'd gotten into that scuffle with a townie the week before. At first, Jake thought he must be buying a drink, but he clutched an empty burlap sack in one hand, and an assortment of items lay spread out on the counter before him. Phoenix and griffin feathers, small bundles of unicorn hairs, wyvern and dragon scales, something in a jar that looked very much like dung, and a great many other things he couldn't identify from where he sat. Walt spoke to the woman behind the bar, and she picked up one of the phoenix feathers and turned it over for examination.

Grace followed his gaze. "He's one of ours, isn't he?" They were only a few feet away from the band, and she had to raise her voice to be heard above the music.

"He is." He watched as the woman—a Caster, not a bartender—set the feather off to the side in a small pile with various other materials. She reached for a bundle of long, silvery unicorn hairs and held them up to the light.

"What's the matter?" Grace asked.

"Nothing. Just surprised to see him here, is all."

"I'm sure he had no idea you'd be here tonight. Anyway, it's not like you didn't already know this was happening."

He nodded. Selling potion ingredients to charm and jinx Casters had always been a good way to make a little extra money, and working on the circus made finding those ingredients easy. Now that the Ban had made such items a highly-restricted commodity, there were even greater profits to be made. Jake couldn't fault the roustabouts for taking advantage of the situation.

So it wasn't a surprise to see Walt bartering with this speakeasy's Caster. Not really. He just hadn't ever expected to see this side of the business up close. The illegal side. The illicit transport and sale of restricted ingredients that had originated from *his* circus. The fact that his business was linked to illegal activity in any way made him uncomfortable, regardless of what his personal views on the matter were.

He was just going to have to get over that discomfort. After all, he was about to purchase and use one of those illegal charms himself, so maybe now wasn't the best time to worry about the moral high ground.

"I'm assuming we just go up there and ask for the charm," he said.

Grace waved a hand dismissively. "Later. Just relax and enjoy the music for a few minutes."

"I thought you said we'd be in and out."

"Oh, come on. You need this. You've been stressing yourself out for weeks now. It's not good for your health."

"I'm more worried about what'll happen to my health if I don't get Burke's money."

She reached across the table and laid her hand over his. "It's going to be all right. Your luck is about to change, but for now, just try to forget about Burke and have a good time."

He slipped his fingers between hers and turned his attention to the band. They'd just finished a song, and the room erupted in applause as they started a new one. Jake leaned back in his chair and tried to banish the tension he'd been carrying around for weeks. After a minute or two, he was swept up in the joy and energy of the music, and his worries and frustrations began to melt away. At least for now.

The spirited tune ended, and he clapped along with the other patrons. When the next song began, Grace stood up and tugged on his hand. "Dance with me."

"I don't know if that's a good idea. This ain't really my kind of dancing music."

"Come on, cowboy, you can't be that bad. And I didn't get all dressed up just to sit here." She pulled him to his feet, and before he had a chance to talk himself out of it, he was following her onto the dance floor.

She rested her hands on his shoulders as he placed his on her waist. He tried his best to match her steps, but he was out of practice and didn't really know what he was doing. She made it look so effortless, but he stumbled through every step.

When he tripped over her foot a second time, she laughed. "You weren't kidding. You're terrible."

"Serves you right for pressuring me to come out here."

"I didn't *pressure* you."

"You absolutely did."

"If that's all it takes to talk you into doing something, I'm going to have to start asking for more favors."

She spun away from him. Jake caught her hand and pulled her back in. Closer this time, so close he could see the amber flecks in her brown eyes. He leaned in to kiss her, then stopped himself when he considered she might not appreciate the display of affection in such a public place.

She lifted her chin and pressed her lips against his. Warmth surged through him and pounded in his heart. Without hesitation, he kissed her back. He didn't care who was watching or what strangers thought of them. Right now, it was just her, just him, and the whole world spinning on without them.

He loved her. He loved her so much it sometimes felt like his heart couldn't carry it all. His grandmother's old wedding ring was buried in a suitcase somewhere on the train, but if it were in his pocket now, he just might be crazy enough to get down on one knee and offer it to her right here.

The song ended, and as they broke apart, she took his hand and gave it a squeeze. "Come on. Let's go get that luck charm of yours."

They made their way to the bar. Walt was nowhere in sight, but the Caster woman he'd been dealing with earlier approached them. "What can I get you folks?"

"We need a luck charm," Grace said. "And why don't you throw in a little boost of charisma while you're at it?"

"Sure thing." She turned to the rows of bottles behind her.

Jake raised an eyebrow. "Charisma, huh?"

"It couldn't hurt."

They ordered drinks while they waited for the Caster to finish her work. The band continued to play as couples twirled across the floor, and Jake and Grace sat hand in hand in comfortable silence.

After a few minutes, the woman returned carrying a small, round bottle filled with a translucent red-orange liquid. She slid it across the counter to them. "There you are. It will go into effect as soon as you take it, but you'll need to use it in the next three days. Lasts about twelve hours. The charisma might wear off a little sooner or later, depending on what you already have to work with."

"Thanks," Grace said. "How much do we owe you?"

"Twenty dollars."

Jake balked at the price, but he took out his billfold and passed the woman four crisp five-dollar bills anyway. Before the Ban, he probably could have bought the same charm for less than half that amount. The woman nodded her thanks and pocketed the money before walking off to serve the next customer.

"Let me see it," Grace said.

Jake handed the bottle over, and she held it up to eye level for inspection.

"Looks right. I wonder if—"

A loud, drawn-out shout from the door cut off whatever she was about to say. "Raid! Everybody out!"

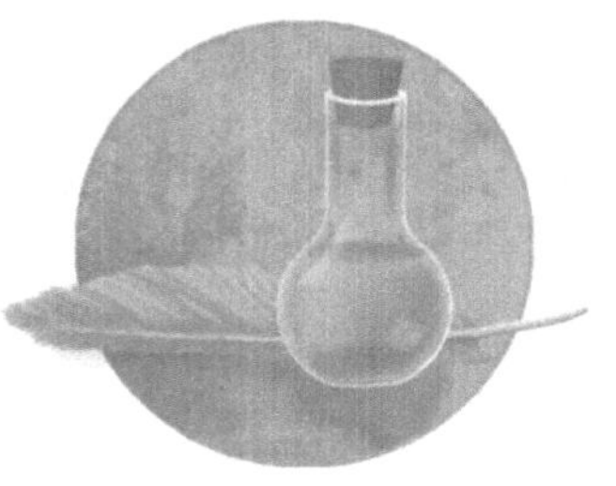

# CHAPTER 10

## ANONYMOUS TIP

A crushing throng of bodies swept past them as people scattered in all directions. Some headed for the shop that served as a cover for the speakeasy while others went for the back-alley door they'd entered through. Grace let out a muffled grunt after a man rushed by and knocked her against the bar. Jake squeezed himself closer to her and put a protective arm around her shoulders.

"You okay?"

She nodded. "Let's just get out of here."

He looked around. Whining sirens and screeching whistles nearly drowned out the panicked cries of his fellow patrons. Uniformed officers poured in through the door that led to the shop, and people began heading for the alley exit en masse.

He grabbed Grace's hand. "Come on."

They had only taken two steps into the crowd when she cried out. "Wait!"

Jake whirled back around as Grace dropped to the floor. She peered through the legs of the people rushing past them, then moved toward something shiny and red on the floor. The luck charm. It must have been knocked from her hands in the chaos.

Jake attempted to shield her from trampling feet as she made her way to the tiny glass bottle. Something strong gripped his arm, and he looked up to see a police officer glaring into his face.

"Put your hands on your head!"

He groaned. Of all the nights he could have chosen to buy an illegal charm, he just had to pick this particular speakeasy on the very same night as a raid.

The officer put a hand on his back and shoved him forward. "Hands on your head. Now!"

Jake interlaced his fingers behind his head and let the officer push him up to the bar. As his face was thrust down onto the polished wood, he glanced over to where Grace had been just moments ago. She wasn't there, but he spotted her near the door, watching him. Her right hand was closed around something small and round, an edge of red just visible at the bottom of her palm.

Her eyes darted from his face to the officers behind him and back again. She took a small, shuffling step forward. But there was nothing she could do. Jake tried to shake his head but found it impossible to move with the officer's forearm pressed down against his neck. Instead, he looked Grace in the eye and mouthed a single word. *Go.*

She gave him an apologetic look, then followed the last stragglers out of the speakeasy and into the night.

♦ ♦ ♦

It was past three o'clock in the morning by the time Jake stumbled back to the circus lot. The police had searched, detained, and questioned him for more than two hours, but ultimately decided to let him go. As he hadn't been in possession of any charms or jinxes, there wasn't much they could charge him with, anyway. Besides, confiscating all the illegal merchandise inside the speakeasy and arresting its owners meant they had bigger fish to fry.

He wanted to check on Grace, so he made his way toward her tent at the far end of the lot. A dark figure shifted against one of the menagerie tent's poles as he walked by. "Have a good night, Jakey boy?" Clarence asked. A fat cigar sat perched between his fangs, its orange glow illuminating his face in grotesque fashion.

Jake kept walking. "Not really."

The ogre stepped out to block his path. "Really? Because you looked pretty happy to me back there, dancing the night away with that pretty friend of yours. You know the one. Animal trainer, spunky little thing. What's her name again?"

"You were there?"

"Of course I was there. Mr. Burke asked me to keep an eye on you, and I take my job very seriously." He took a long drag of his cigar and blew the smoke out over Jake's head. "Besides, we all have to do our civic duty from time to time, don't we? Make sure there isn't any criminal activity going on in our peaceful neighborhoods."

Jake's throat felt like cotton. "The raid—that was you. You called the police."

Clarence shrugged. "I believe it was an anonymous tip."

"Anonymous, my ass. What's it matter to you how I choose to get Burke's money?"

"That's *Mr.* Burke. And you're wasting your time. That luck charm wouldn't have done you any good, anyway."

He spoke of the charm as if Jake no longer had it, and judging by the smile on his face, that seemed to please him. Maybe because that was what he'd intended to happen when he'd contacted the police.

Or maybe because he'd confiscated the charm from Grace when she'd returned here.

He'd learn the truth once he found her, but there was still something about Clarence's actions that nagged at him. "Look, if you wanna keep an eye on me, that's fine. But I don't see how you interfering in my business with your boss is good for either of us."

Clarence blew out another puff of smoke, slow and casual. "I guess we'll find out, won't we?"

Jake shook his head. He had better things to worry about than trying to decipher Clarence's riddles. "Excuse me."

The ogre stepped aside with a dramatic flourish and allowed Jake to pass.

He quickened his pace, eager to reach Grace's tent and find out what had happened to the luck charm. She was sitting on the edge of her cot when he stepped inside. The moment she saw him, she stood and threw her arms around his neck. Her breath was warm against his skin. "Oh, good. You're all right."

"Yeah. And you?" He took a step back to look her over. She'd thrown a light jacket over her dress, and much of her hair had come loose from its bun, but she appeared to be unharmed.

"I'm fine," she said. "What happened?"

"The police held me up for a little while, and then I ran into Clarence on the way here. Do you still have the charm?"

She reached into the pocket of her jacket and pulled it out. "Of course. Why?"

"Clarence seemed to think I lost it. I was worried he might have taken it from you."

"He asked about it when I got back. He was pretty insistent, right up until I offered to let him search me himself."

"You did *what*?"

"Don't worry, he didn't actually do it. As soon as I suggested it, he got all flustered and apologetic. I can't believe I'm saying this, but in some ways, he's almost a gentleman. Or he likes to think of himself that way, at least."

Jake stifled a laugh. Clarence, a gentleman? The suits, cigars, and fancy watch could only do so much, but maybe he really was aiming for his best approximation of class and refinement.

"At least the charm is safe," she said. "And you're safe. That's all that matters."

"Do you really think it'll work?"

She pressed the bottle into his palm and clasped his hand in both of hers. "I really hope so."

# CHAPTER 11

## A CHANGE IN LUCK

Jake spent what little was left of that night with Grace. She drifted off in his arms as they lay squeezed together on her tiny cot, but he couldn't sleep himself. When the first light of dawn crept into the tent, he carefully disentangled himself from her and slipped on his boots. She stirred for a moment, then went back to sleep. After planting a light kiss on her cheek and checking to make sure the luck charm was still in his pocket, he picked up his hat and headed back to his train car for a change of clothes.

Clarence was mercifully absent when he arrived. Wherever he'd gone, Jake didn't care. The less he had to see of the ogre, the happier he'd be.

He picked out his new clothes and started to undress. When he removed his pants, the luck charm fell out of his pocket and rolled over to the bed. He sat down and picked up the small bottle. Twelve hours, the Caster had said. Twelve hours to change his luck and his fate. It was the dawn of a new day. No better time to start than now.

It couldn't actually be that easy, could it?

Last night, he'd been desperate enough to believe a simple charm really could make all the difference in solving his problems. Now, he wasn't so sure. But he had to do something, and this was as good an option as any.

He uncorked the bottle and swirled its contents around a few times. It had a light, sweet smell. He raised the bottle to his lips and took a tentative sip. When he tasted honey, he drank the rest in two quick gulps and waited for it to take effect.

After a few minutes, he felt…nothing. No surge of power, no sudden impression that he could take on the world, not even a mildly boosted sense of optimism. He wasn't exactly sure what he was supposed to feel, but he should have felt *something*. Shouldn't he?

Rumors had long circulated that some bootleggers and speakeasies watered down their charms and jinxes to increase profits and keep up with the demand for products. There was no one to regulate the business, after all, which meant they could do whatever they pleased.

All the last hopes he'd been clinging to fizzled out.

He'd been scammed. This wasn't a luck charm at all, just a jar of colored, flavored water he'd paid way too much for. He couldn't go back to the establishment to complain, and even if he could, it wasn't like there was any real way to distinguish good luck from the absence of good luck. He'd been a fool to ever think this could work.

He pressed his palms against his eye sockets and ran his fingers through his hair, cursing himself, his father, Burke, Clarence, the Caster at the bar, and everyone else he could think of who'd had anything to do with this.

When he looked up, he spotted something unusual in the small mirror stuck to the wall in front of him. Instead of his own face, the mirror reflected the heavily made-up features of Alexandra Armstrong. She waved as she caught his eye, then pointed to something and covered her mouth with her hand like she was trying to hide a laugh.

Jake suddenly remembered he was sitting on the edge of his bed in his underwear.

He swore, grabbed his pants, and hurried to put his legs through them. He stood to pull them up, nearly tripping himself in the process.

So much for good luck.

The worn shirt he grabbed next wasn't exactly the most presentable thing for a conversation with a colleague, but it would have to do for now. Alexandra's voice became audible as he reached out to touch the mirror, still fighting his buttons with the other hand.

"Oh relax, dear. It's nothing I haven't seen before."

He felt like he should apologize anyway. "Sorry."

"No, it's my fault. I shouldn't have tried to reach you so early."

She seemed awfully sunny compared to the last time they'd spoken. If she was still mad at him, she didn't show it, and he wasn't about to remind her. "What can I do for you?"

"I hear you're still looking for a buyer for your basilisk."

"We are. Were you still interested?" Did he dare let himself hope?

"Oliver and I talked it over, and I think I may have been a little too harsh with you the last time we spoke."

Jake seized the opportunity to mend the bridges he'd burned. "No, ma'am. I was in the wrong. I never should have broken our agreement, and I'm sorry."

"I appreciate that. We really do want the basilisk, though we can't offer you as much as we'd agreed on before."

She knew he couldn't afford to turn her down no matter how much the offer was. But maybe there was still a way they could both get what they wanted. "Would you do it if I threw in something else?"

Alexandra cocked her head to one side. "Like what?"

"Our illusionist hasn't been the best fit for our show. She's got about seven months left on her contract, but I'm willing to transfer it over to you if you'll buy the basilisk for nine thousand like we agreed before."

"You would give up Madame Arabella? She's a star."

"To be honest, she's a little too high-strung for me."

Alexandra's smile spread across her entire face. "Oh, I can work with high-strung. You've got yourself a deal."

Jake could hardly believe what he was hearing. He'd given up on ever selling the basilisk to anyone, especially Alexandra and Oliver Armstrong. Maybe he shouldn't have been so happy to be losing one of his best performers, but with the way things had been going so far, he considered it a small price to pay.

"We've got your schedule," Alexandra said. "I'll send a few of my men to collect the beast before next week, and we'll get a train ticket for Madame Arabella."

"I'll let her know. Thank you."

"A pleasure doing business with you."

When she was gone, he lowered himself back onto the edge of the bed. Did that really just happen? It felt too good to be true, like something out of a dream, but it was too real to be a dream. He eyed the now-empty bottle sitting next to his pillow with new appreciation and renewed hope. He'd gotten lucky. Inexplicably, irrationally, wonderfully lucky.

Now to see how far that charm could carry him.

♦ ♦ ♦

By the time the sun went down that night, Jake had managed to sell a hippogriff, four wyverns, two phoenixes, four giant spiders, a pair of unicorns, several camels, three elephants, and the wagons and draft horses he would no longer need to transport them. Workmen would be coming to collect the purchases and give Jake his money over the course of the next week. Most of the shows he'd sold to had ended up paying at least as much as he'd originally asked for, and in a few cases even more. The luck charm had worked even better than he expected.

As the train rolled along the tracks on its way to their next show, he met Grace in the stock car that housed Trigger, Bullseye, and Calico Thunder. Between his business dealings, her practicing a new set of tricks with the animals, and the day's two performances, they hadn't had a chance to talk since last night, and Jake was dying to tell her about his success. *Their* success, since the luck charm had been her idea in the first place.

"It worked," he said once they were alone together. "I still can't believe it, but it actually *worked*."

She listened as he rattled off a list of all the creatures and equipment he'd sold and to whom and for how much. When he was finished, she took his hand and squeezed it. "That's great, Jake. Really great." But her voice sounded hollow, and the expression she bore was devoid of its usual animated vibrance. She turned her face away from him and stared at the floor.

He clasped her hand in both of his and pulled her a little closer. "What's wrong?"

"Nothing."

"Please, look at me."

She did. Her eyelashes were wet with newly-formed tears.

His stomach dropped, and he reached up to cup her face in one hand. "Oh, Grace. I'm a damn fool. I'm so sorry."

She shook her head. "It's not your fault."

"I shouldn't have said all that stuff, carrying on like I'm some kind of hero when all I've really done is gutted this show and sold the pieces to the highest bidder."

This show. Her home. The only home she'd ever known.

"It's not your fault," she said again. The tears in her eyes brimmed over and began to run down her cheeks. "If anyone gutted us, it was Cliff, and he did it long before you got here."

The pain in her voice was tangible, reminiscent of some of Jake's own childhood memories. He thought he understood a little of what she was feeling, but he wasn't sure what to say. He'd learned a long time ago that the man he wanted his father to be was only an illusion, but for Grace, Cliff Strickland had been a hero. And it was never easy to learn your heroes were messy and imperfect, no matter how long the signs had been there.

"I'm sorry," he said again, this time apologizing for both himself and his father. "I'm sure he never meant for any of this to happen."

Grace snorted and shook her head. "Of course he didn't. To be honest, I'm not sure he ever meant for *anything* to happen. He never planned ahead, never thought about the future. He just lived for the moment and did whatever he wanted, consequences be damned."

She pulled away from him and wiped her tears with her sleeve, then took Cliff's old pocketknife out of her skirt. She turned it over in her hands as she leaned against the railing of Calico Thunder's pen. "You know, when you first came here, I hated you. I hated you before you even got here, from the moment Cliff told me you were coming. And then you showed up, and you were...nothing like I expected."

"What were you expecting?"

She shrugged. "Horns. Cloven hooves. Maybe a tail."

"That bad, huh?"

"Can you blame me? I know he wasn't the father you deserved, but he was for me. When my mom died and my dad took off, he made up for both of them. But then he was so excited about you coming—his real son. And how could I ever hope to compete with that?"

Jake leaned against the railing next to her and clasped his hands together. The cruel irony was that she *had* competed with that, for years, without ever knowing it. And won. She was part of the circus, and the circus had been the only family Cliff ever really wanted. His own flesh and blood—his *real* son, as she had put it—well, he'd never been any more real to Cliff than the hard practicalities and responsibilities of running his business.

"Like I said, I hated you," Grace went on. "Or I told myself I did. Really, I think I was just jealous."

"Would it make you feel any better if I told you I was jealous of you?"

"A little." She gave him a small smile. "Anyway, I stopped trying to hate you after a few months, and I stopped being jealous once I really got to know you. But *damn* if it didn't all come back the day he told us he was dying and planned to leave the show to you."

Jake remembered. The argument that followed had been one of their first, but it was still by far their worst. Funny thing was the argument hadn't even started over the circus. It had taken him weeks to realize that was exactly what the fight had been about for Grace, though, even if she hadn't said it in words.

"He should've left it all to you."

"He should have," she agreed resolutely. "Instead, all I got was his old, dull pocketknife. I've lived on this train practically my whole life, and you were just some First of May cowboy who didn't even want to be here most days. It made no sense."

"That's what I told him. Anyone but me. He wouldn't listen. Kept insisting he 'owed me something' for all the years he wasn't around."

"That was part of it, I'm sure. But after all this, I wonder if he had other reasons."

"You mean like protecting you?" The thought had crossed his mind a time or two before.

She nodded and stared down at the knife in her hands with a wistful look in her eye. "He was always trying to protect me. He had to have known Burke would come for his money sooner or later. Money we didn't have. And instead of leaving the mess for me to clean up…"

"He left it to me." He shook his head and sighed. "Even for him, that's a pretty low blow."

"It is. Asshole."

Jake laughed. Such words for his father had come out of his mouth on more than one occasion, but never hers. She'd rarely even so much as criticized Cliff for anything, and now she was jumping straight from criticism to cussing him out.

She nudged his shoulder with hers. "I'm glad you're finding a way to fix his mistakes, even if I'm not happy about the way it has to happen."

"I wish it didn't have to get any worse." He shook his head. "Even after everything I sold today, I ain't got all the money I need."

"You mean you're going to hold everyone's wages?"

"I don't have much choice. I'll have to tell them tomorrow." Maybe he should have told them sooner, but a small part of him had still been holding out hope that it wouldn't come to that. "It's gonna be ugly."

"Maybe I can soften the blow a little."

"I'd appreciate that." He yawned and pushed himself up off the railing. "I'd better hit the sack. They really oughta warn you about the exhaustion that comes as a side effect of that luck charm."

"I think that has more to do with the fact that you were up so late last night dancing. Or, you know, whatever it was you want to call that."

"Hey, now. Don't knock my dancing, or I might never go out with you out again."

"Liar."

He gave her a quick kiss. "I'll see you tomorrow."

"Hey, Jake?" She grabbed his hand before he could walk away. "I'm glad Cliff gave the circus to you instead of me. Not just because of this business with the mob. You really turned things around when you took over. You saved us, and even if it means we only got a couple more good years on the show, it was worth it."

The pressing weight in his chest lightened just a little. "Goodnight, Grace."

"Goodnight."

# CHAPTER 12

## MAKING ENEMIES

Jake waited until after the parade the next morning to break the bad news to his employees. The vast majority of them were gathered in the cookhouse to eat, but he hadn't bothered to grab a plate. His stomach felt queasy already, and he doubted that would change once he said what he needed to say and made enemies of just about everyone around him.

But there was no avoiding the situation, so he might as well get on with it. He gave Grace's hand a quick squeeze under the table, then stood on top of his chair and cleared his throat. "Could I get everyone's attention for a minute?"

The hubbub continued until Bruno stuck his fingers in his mouth and let out a sharp whistle. Scattered conversations fizzled out, and soon every face turned to Jake.

"Thank you." His heart hammered against his chest, and he sucked in a deep breath before continuing. "I know there have been rumors going around that we're struggling financially. I wish I could say it's just gossip, but that wouldn't be very honest. Truth is, we are in a bit of trouble. Things have come up that I wasn't expecting, and because of that, I've been forced to downsize our show."

A low murmur spread through the tent as they took in his words. He waited for them to settle before continuing. "I've sold some of the animals and equipment, so people will be coming to pick up their purchases starting this afternoon. Unfortunately, that still won't be enough to take care of our problem, so I'm gonna have to do something I promised you all I'd do my best to avoid. I have to hold wages, at least for a few weeks. For everyone—performers, too. There's just no way around it."

The murmur rose to a clamor of heated objections and indignant shouts. Bruno's face stood out among the rest, betrayal apparent in his wounded expression. Jake hated himself for the lies he'd told his friend, for reassuring him over and over again that there was nothing to worry about when that wasn't the case at all. He'd justified his actions because he thought he'd been protecting Bruno, but he'd also done it to protect himself. All he wanted was to jump down from his chair and disappear, but he stood firm where he was.

As he looked out at the sea of angry faces before him, his eyes met Clarence's. The ogre returned his gaze with an amused smile, shrugged one shoulder, and took a long drink from his tin cup.

Grace shouted something, but her words were inaudible over the tumult. She climbed up onto the table next to Jake and called out again. "Hey! Listen up!" It took a while, but the noise eventually died down enough to let her speak. "Look, this isn't what any of us wanted to hear, but Jake's right. I've been over the numbers with him. He has no other choice."

Murmurs began to rise up again, but Grace shot a few icy glances in the direction of those conversations to silence them. "More importantly," she went on, "this isn't his fault. Cliff poured his heart into this show, but he always had a bigger imagination than he had common sense. We were going bankrupt long before Jake took over, and he's done everything he can to fix things since then. Those of you who've been here long enough should remember that."

After a few seconds, Otto stood up from his chair. "She's right," he called out. "The lad's pulled us through worse than this, and he's never done us wrong before. If he says this is the only way, I trust him."

Some of the others nodded. Many, Bruno included, remained sullen and disgruntled. But at least they weren't yelling anymore.

"I'm sorry," Jake said, hoping the genuine regret he felt would carry to them through his voice. "If there was any other way to fix this, I'd do it. I know it ain't fair, but it's what's necessary to keep the show running."

"How long before we get paid?" someone asked.

"I can't say yet, but I'm doing the best I can. I'll try to pay at least part of what I owe you next month."

"That's the best we can ask for," Grace said.

There was nothing left to say. Jake hopped down from the table, and the usual chatter in the cookhouse resumed, albeit with a darker tone than before. He turned to Grace. "Well, that could have gone worse. Thanks for backing me up."

"I only spoke the truth."

A beefy hand fell on his shoulder, and he looked up to see Clarence standing over him. "Bravo on that speech, Jakey boy. You really pissed them off. Some of Otto's men are already packing their bags to seek their fortunes elsewhere."

He wasn't surprised. He wasn't even disappointed. With everything he'd sold and the show's downsizing, there would be far less work for the roustabouts by next week. If enough of them left voluntarily, he wouldn't have to lay off so many of them later.

Clarence tightened his grip on Jake's shoulder and leaned in closer, his lips curled in a sneer. "Show starts in a few hours. Do you really expect any of them to perform their best after that?"

Grace watched him lumber off with a steely glare. "All the time he's been here, and he still hasn't figured out we're tougher than we look. A tiny setback like this isn't enough to stop the show."

"Maybe not for the rest of you," Jake said, "but I wouldn't speak for Madame Arabella."

The star illusionist was already marching toward him, her chin held high and her chest thrust out. Not wanting to have this particular conversation in such a public place, he stood and left the cookhouse at a brisk walk.

As expected, Madame Arabella followed, calling his name in a loud screech and repeating it when he pretended he couldn't hear her. He reached a more secluded spot outside the big top and turned around to face her. Her face was flushed, her thin lips puckered, and she nearly tripped in her ridiculously high heels as she hurried to catch him.

"Good morning, ma'am," he said. "What can I do for you?"

"I think you know perfectly well what I need from you, Mr. Strickland. If you think for one second you can withhold *my* wages, you're out of your mind. The rest of these poor saps may be willing to put up with your outrageous stunt, but I most certainly am not. In case you've forgotten, my father is a lawyer, and he—"

Jake held up a hand to interrupt her tirade. "Now, hold on just a minute. I've already made other arrangements I think you'll be pleased with."

"Arrangements? What sort of arrangements?"

"I transferred your contract."

Her nostrils flared. "You transferred my—what makes you think can just—"

"To the Armstrong Family Circus."

Her expression shifted immediately, and her voice became as sweet as honey as she looked at him with wide, bright eyes. "The Armstrongs? Truly?"

Jake simply nodded.

Before he could stop her, Madame Arabella threw her arms around his shoulders and planted a big, sloppy kiss on his cheek. "Oh, thank you, Mr. Strickland. What a wonderful opportunity. I knew I could count on you."

He struggled to tactfully extricate himself from her embrace and the stifling, multilayered fabric of her dress. If she knew he'd only thrown in her contract to sweeten the deal on the basilisk, she might have slapped him instead, but this wasn't much better. In his desperation to escape her grasp, he was tempted to tell her the truth. Thankfully, she released him before he was forced to resort to that.

"Some of the men from their show are coming in a few days," Jake said. "They've bought you a train ticket so you can go back with them after they pick up their other purchases."

Madame Arabella beamed. "Oh, this is such wonderful news! I must tell my father."

She turned and walked away with a new flounce in her step, leaving Jake with a profound sense of relief. He had enough on his plate already without having to worry about the complaints and demands of a spoiled prima donna. The Armstrongs could have her, and good riddance.

He'd barely begun to savor that relief when a new complication materialized. Bruno marched toward him with all the fury of an enraged bull, his mouth set in a hard, downturned line. "What in the name of all blazing forge-fires was that?"

"I'm sorry, Bruno. I just—"

"*Sorry?* How many times did I ask you? How many times did you lie to my face and tell me there was nothing to worry about?"

"I wanted to tell you, but I couldn't."

Bruno crossed his arms. "Fine, then. Tell me now. What's this really about?"

"It's better if you don't know."

His face flushed an even deeper red. "And you think you have the right to decide that? You trusted me enough to help you strip this show, but not enough to tell me why or how bad it was."

He stuck his hands in his pockets and repeated the same worthless apology. "I'm sorry."

Bruno shook his head. "Tell you what, Jake, the next time you need a favor from a friend, don't come knocking on my door." With that, he turned on his heel and marched away, the tails of his red coat flapping behind him.

Jake took a few steps after him as guilt pinched his chest, then stopped himself and stuffed the feeling down. Bruno had every right to be upset, but he was looking for answers Jake couldn't give him. Trying to reason with him now wasn't going to do any good and would probably just upset him more. Besides, he had bigger problems to worry about, and Bruno would come around. Eventually.

At least, he hoped so.

# CHAPTER 13

## A SHOW OF GOOD FAITH

"I need to meet with Burke," Jake said to Clarence a few nights later as the train departed for the show's next stand.

The ogre raised an eyebrow but didn't look up from the newspaper he was reading. "Is that so? I'm almost certain you don't have all his money yet. So what, pray tell, do you need to see him for?"

"That's between me and him."

Tomorrow, the last of the workmen from other shows would come to pay him and collect their purchases, and with the deadline Burke had established just ten days away, it was time to renegotiate the terms of their arrangement. Jake had done all the calculations this morning. Between the money he'd collected through ticket sales, selling off parts of the circus, and holding everyone's wages, he had a little more than a hundred and fifty thousand dollars right now. Less than half of what he owed Burke, but he'd made a valiant effort. Hopefully, the mobster would agree to some kind of long-term repayment plan.

It was the only rational option, really. For both of them. Despite Burke's threats, he needed Jake alive. He couldn't collect money from a dead man.

Clarence folded up his newspaper and raised one foot to rest on his other knee. "I don't know, Jakey boy. Are you sure that's a good idea? Mr. Burke isn't someone you just request a meeting with whenever you feel like it."

"He wants his money, don't he?"

The ogre gave him a curious look and shrugged. "All right, then. But don't say I didn't warn you."

From his pocket, he pulled out a fountain pen and a half-sheet of paper that had been torn down the middle. Words were scribbled across the entire front side of the page and a small portion of the back, and Clarence wrote something down under the last line. The messages already scrawled over its surface were likely reports to Burke, who must have the other half of the page. Enchanted paper was a common means of correspondence and cheaper than paying an Enchanter for face-to-face mirror communication.

The ogre capped his pen and turned to Jake. "There, I've put in your request."

"How long will it take him to respond?"

"It depends. Not too long, I imagine."

Jake sat down on the edge of his bed. He took out the route book and a pen of his own to jot a few notes about the day's performance, but once that was done, he had nothing to do but wait. His foot bounced up and down against the floor to the rhythm of the train's clattering along the tracks. He'd been so confident about meeting with Burke a few hours ago. Now, he wondered if Clarence was right. Maybe this was a terrible idea.

But it wasn't like he had any other options. There was no way he could get the rest of Burke's money in a week. This would have to be enough for now. And if it wasn't...well, he would cross that bridge when he came to it, or drown trying.

Clarence picked up the sheet of paper again and held it up to read, but Jake was too far away to make out the new words that had appeared. The ogre nodded to himself, then wrote something else down and returned the paper and pen to his pocket.

"Well?" Jake said.

"You're doing a two-day stand in Griffinsburg in a few days, right? Mr. Burke says he'll meet us there."

"What time? Where?"

"Not sure. He'll send a car to pick us up." He unfolded his newspaper and went back to reading. "If I were you, I'd start praying he's in a good mood when you see him."

♦ ♦ ♦

The evening of their first day in Griffinsburg, Jake and Clarence climbed into the back of the shiny black town car Burke sent for them. The driver was none other than Sean, Clarence's shorter, thicker counterpart, and the two exchanged a few grunted words in some ogre dialect Jake didn't recognize. He patted the worn leather travel bag on his lap with one hand to reassure himself that its contents were still there. Nothing had happened that might make him think otherwise, but one hundred and fifty thousand dollars was a lot of money, and just carrying it around gave him an odd, jittery sense of vulnerability.

The sun hung low in the sky, a bright, orange circle casting long shadows across the ground. He looked out the window and watched the big top grow smaller in one of the side mirrors. Right now, Bruno was probably announcing Grace and her extraordinary winged beasts to come out to the center ring to the roar of a cheering crowd.

Jake would have much rather been there watching her, and she'd wanted to come with him to this meeting with Burke. But with Madame Arabella gone, they couldn't afford to cut another of their best acts, even for one show, so she'd stayed behind. Better that way, anyhow. He didn't like the idea of her getting any more tangled up in this than she already was.

They drove through the streets of Griffinsburg at a leisurely speed. It was a big city—one of the biggest they'd scheduled for their summer tour. Billboards advertising everything from cigarettes to automobiles rose up over building rooftops, and the brightly lit storefronts below competed for the attention and patronage of passersby. Women in cloches and men wearing bowlers and flat caps walked the sidewalks at a brisk pace as they went about their business. A throng of people milled about outside a theater, its marquee adorned with bold letters proclaiming the title and stars of that night's silent film. Somewhere nearby, a lone trumpet player riffed a few notes.

Sean drove the car down a narrow, one-way street and pulled up to the curb outside a brick building. Clarence got out first and held the door open for Jake. He exited the vehicle and followed the two ogres inside the establishment, which turned out to be a restaurant.

A few people sat at the booths lining the walls, but the place was mostly empty. Clarence and Sean nodded to the host at the front door and headed straight for the kitchen. Jake hurried along after them, his bag clutched tight in one fist.

His stomach rumbled as they passed by the grill, where a man in a white apron was frying chicken. The scent brought back flashes of his childhood—cold winter days spent sitting on a stool in the kitchen while Ma cooked and sang to him. But there was no time for reminiscing now. He shoved away the nostalgia that washed over him and kept following the two ogres.

Clarence opened the steel door to what looked like a refrigeration room, but instead, they stepped through to a secret bar. It was fancier than the last such joint Jake had been to, with a few chandeliers hanging from the ceiling and red velvet curtains draped over the walls. A jazz quartet played in the corner while a woman in a beaded dress sang a bluesy song about loss and heartbreak. Her audience consisted of the bartender, a lone couple dancing on a hardwood floor, and a man in a gray fedora sitting on a barstool.

The man spun around on his stool as they entered. It was Burke, wearing his true face this time rather than some elaborate glamour. When he saw Jake, his face lit up like he was reuniting with an old friend for the first time in years. He gestured to the completely empty row of barstools to either side of him and called out over the music. "Jake! You made it. Come have a seat. I saved you a spot."

Jake set his bag on the ground and took the barstool next to him. Sean and Clarence found seats at a nearby table.

Burke clapped a hand on Jake's shoulder. "I apologize for the atmosphere. It's usually a little more lively in here, but with the circus in town, I'm afraid business is slow. More ticket sales for you though, right? There's no denying you need it." He elbowed Jake in the ribs and winked. "Can I get you something to drink? It's on the house."

"No thanks, I'm fine."

"Are you sure?" Burke asked. "We have just about anything you could want. And if you're looking for something a little stronger than alcohol, Louis here can mix some pretty impressive charms. Maybe you're due for another boost of luck?"

"That's all right."

The bartender shrugged and went back to rearranging the bottles behind the counter.

Burke cocked an eyebrow at Jake and swirled his own drink around in the glass. "So, Clarence says you have something important to discuss with me."

Jake bent to pick up his leather bag from the floor and handed it over. "It's your money. Not all of it, but a pretty fair portion, considering the time constraints."

Burke unzipped the bag and pulled it open just far enough to peer at the stacks of bills inside. He didn't say anything for a while, and Jake wasn't sure if he was counting or just mulling things over. Whatever it was, he didn't dare interrupt.

"How much?" Burke said at last.

"A hundred and fifty thousand. Like I said, it's not everything. I just wanted to give it to you as a show of good faith."

"A show of good faith," Burke repeated flatly.

"Yessir." He leaned forward and shifted a little toward the man. "Look, I've done everything I could to come up with that money. If you don't believe me, ask Clarence."

Burke called over his shoulder. "Is that right, Clarence? Has Jake been working hard to get our money?"

The ogre chuckled. "Working like a dog."

"Like a dog." Burke's voice was low and quiet in a way that seemed to suck the life right out of everything in the room, even the music. He set the bag on the empty bar stool beside him and turned to Jake. "Let me ask you something. What exactly were you hoping to get out of this meeting?"

His words hung in the air like a challenge—a challenge Jake could never hope to win. Coming here had been a mistake. But he was out of options, and he had nowhere to go and nothing to say except to answer the mobster's question.

He swallowed the saliva that had been building up in the back of his throat. "I was hoping you might be willing to give me a little more time. Maybe we could work out some kind of business arrangement."

"I had a business arrangement with your father. Look where that got me. Why should I trust the word of another Strickland?"

"With all due respect, Mr. Burke, I ain't my father. I'm barely even his son. In fact, I'm half convinced he only gave me his circus as one last way to screw with me, or maybe to screw with both of us. But I'm an honest, hardworking man, and I promise I'll make every single payment until this debt's gone. There's just no way I can get the rest of the money by next week. It's impossible."

Burke stared back at him without saying a single word, leaving Jake to interpret his silence and the thoughts that lay behind it. Was he angry? That seemed likely, given Jake had barely managed to obtain a third of the sum his father owed. But what could he really expect? It was an enormous amount of money. The arrangement Jake was offering wasn't perfect, but it was in both of their best interests. Surely Burke was rational enough to see that.

After what felt like an eternity, the mobster reached into the bag Jake had given him and took a single hundred-dollar bill off the top. He slid it across the counter to the bartender and stood up from his stool. "Take a walk with me, Jake."

His legs shook, but he followed Burke past Clarence and Sean's table, past the band and the dancing couple to a door at the back of the room. It was a different door than they'd entered through, and it exited out to a narrow alley sandwiched between two brick buildings. Discarded cans, bottles, and papers were smashed up against the base of the walls, and a dark grime obscured some of the cobblestones. The sky had turned a dusky gray while they were inside, and the glow of a few flashing signs reflected off the water pooled in a gutter that ran down the center of the alley.

It was exactly the sort of place Jake didn't want to find himself in alone with an infamous criminal after dark.

But they weren't alone. He turned to look for an escape and instead saw Sean and Clarence looming above him. The man who'd been dancing with the girl inside stood between them, a greasy smirk stretching his lips across crooked yellow teeth.

Burke threw an arm over his shoulder. "Listen, Jake. I like you. And I can tell you worked hard trying to get that money. I appreciate that, I really do."

It wasn't exactly how he'd expected this conversation to go, and he started to relax a little. Maybe Burke was going to be sensible about this after all.

"And," he went on, "you were man enough to come and talk to me when you realized you had a problem. See, that's the kind of honesty I can respect in a person. It's something I wish your father had shown me. If he'd been up-front about any trouble he was having with his payments, I'm sure he would have found me reasonable. I am a reasonable man, aren't I, boys?"

"Very reasonable, sir," Clarence agreed.

"*Very* reasonable. But I'm also a man who values respect. It's a cruel world out here, you know that. I have my own financial problems, my own family to take care of, my own businesses to run. So I respect you, Jake, I really do. But if I go around making exceptions and special arrangements for every poor sap who owes me money, people are going to stop respecting *me*. And that's something I just can't have."

He stopped walking and took a pack of cigarettes and a lighter out of his suit pocket. It produced a flame on the second try, and the orange light illuminated his face like some kind of hellish demon in the shadows.

Jake's heart started to pound, and his muscles clenched in preparation for what he knew was coming next. Nowhere to run, nowhere to hide, just him and four mobsters in some dirty back alley where no one was coming to help him.

Burke puffed on his cigarette and casually blew the smoke out in a ring. "Please don't take this personally. It's just business."

He gave a nod to his three lackeys, but Jake was ready. He whirled around just in time to see—and dodge—a blow aimed at his head. He lashed out with his own strike, and his fist connected with Clarence's stomach.

The ogre didn't even grunt. Instead, he raised his foot and sent it hurtling into Jake's chest.

He flew back and hit the ground, barely managing to keep his head up so it didn't smack against the cobblestones. Before he could recover his breath, Sean and the man from the dance floor were above him.

He tried to skitter backwards, but his foot slipped in a patch of gutter slime and put him flat on his back. Pain screamed up his spine, then across his ribcage as someone kicked him, then again on the other side when a second blow fell. He curled into a ball with his arms over his head.

There were three of them, and the two ogres were twice his size. Fighting back was pointless. All he could do now was hope it ended quickly.

It didn't. After a few more kicks, someone grabbed him by the shirt and hauled him up onto his feet. One of them held his arms from behind. He flailed as the other two took turns punching him in the face, the stomach, the ribs, the spine. Their faces spun in front of him, soon becoming indistinguishable from one another.

Everything was throbbing, biting, electrifying agony.

Someone kicked his kneecap, and he gave up on any attempts to support his own weight. The person holding his arms let him fall, and this time, he didn't have the wherewithal to stop his skull from cracking against the ground. A new burst of pain exploded like firecrackers inside his head. Through the narrow field of vision in his swollen left eye, he watched his own blood seep into the cracks between the cobblestones, but he couldn't tell where it was coming from.

A cigarette butt dropped to the ground in front of his face, followed by a shiny wingtip shoe stepping on it to snuff it out. The shoe's owner crouched down next to him, and Burke's face slowly came into focus.

"You have one week to get the rest of my money, Jake. No extensions, no exceptions. If you don't have it the next time we see each other, we won't just beat you within an inch of your life. We'll beat the life right out of you *and* that pretty little dragon trainer you seem to be so fond of."

Jake let out an animalistic roar and scrabbled for Burke's leg, but he couldn't quite reach him. If they harmed even a single hair on Grace's head, he'd kill them. He'd kill every last one of them.

Even in his head, the threat felt empty and pathetic. He was just a broken cowboy in a lonely alley with no power and no resources. They had won. No matter what he did, they would always win.

Burke stood up. "Still got a little fight in you. That's good. Use it to get the rest of my money. I'm sure you'll figure something out."

They left him lying on the ground, battered and bruised, with both his blood and his pride slowly draining out into the dirty gutter beneath him.

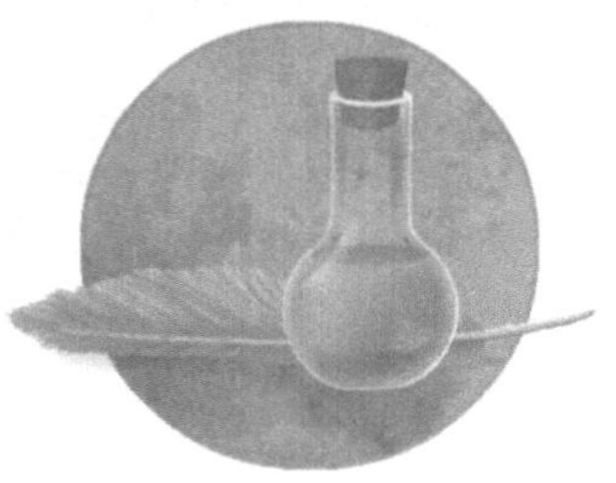

# CHAPTER 14

## HEALER'S TOUCH

Minutes passed before Jake managed to pick himself up off the ground, his body protesting every movement. He put one hand against the wall of a building for support as he hobbled down the alley to the adjoining street, but the ground still seemed to lurch beneath his feet. His back hurt worst of all. A jolting pain radiated from the lower vertebrae he'd injured riding dragons years before, so intense he doubted even Grace's potions would be able to do much to ease his suffering.

He had to get back. She'd worry if he wasn't back soon.

He kept walking, each step slow and painful. Burke and his men were nowhere in sight. Even Clarence had gone, and the residents of Griffinsburg simply continued to go about their business under the bright city lights. A few of them glanced his way and grimaced when they saw his injured face and disheveled clothes, but no one stopped to offer help.

He made his way to the edge of the sidewalk and hailed a cab. "Where are you headed?" the driver asked as he climbed inside.

"Strickland's Circus." His voice sounded garbled and distant, maybe because of the ringing in his ears and the pounding in his head, or maybe because his swollen mouth couldn't form words properly. "They're on a lot on the east end of town."

"Yeah, I know where the circus is. Show's over, though, you know. At least until tomorrow. Is there somewhere else I can take you?" He turned around, and his eyes widened as he got a good look at Jake for the first time. "You need to go to the hospital, mister. I'll take you. I won't even charge you for the ride."

"No. Just get me to the circus."

"I think you're in worse shape than you realize. You really ought to let someone have a look at you."

Jake reached for the door handle. The last thing he needed right now was some teenaged cabbie giving him advice.

The boy reached out and put a hand on his shoulder. "Now, hold on there, mister, don't leave. You want to get to the circus, I'll take you to the circus. All right? Just stay in the car." He shook his head and muttered to himself. "Just trying to help a guy out."

The car pulled forward, and Jake gingerly leaned his head against the window. The cool glass was soothing against his skin and seemed to ease the ache in his skull. After a few minutes, he drifted into the blissful numbness of sleep.

A touch on his shoulder startled him awake. He flinched, and the cabbie jerked his hand back. "Sorry to wake you, but we're here."

Jake straightened up and peered out the window. They were in front of the ticket booth, and it was a long walk from there to the sleeping tents behind the dressing rooms. A long walk with plenty of people to see him on the way. "Drive around to the back of the big top."

"Oh, I don't think I'm allowed to do that."

"It's my circus, and this lot is ours until tomorrow. You can go wherever I say you can."

A question formed in the boy's eyes, but he was polite enough not to ask it and put his hands back on the wheel. Jake slumped down in his seat to avoid being seen through the windows.

They circled around the big top to the smaller dressing room tent. Behind that, several of the performers had set up their own tents and cots for the overnight stop. Lantern light illuminated the largest of them, and the silhouettes of the people inside danced on the canvas like shadow puppets. Jake pointed it out to the cabbie. "Stop right there."

As the car came to rest, he pulled out his billfold, then hesitated. He couldn't walk in there looking like this. "Could I get you to do me one more favor?"

"What?"

"Go into that tent and see if you can find a woman named Grace. Bring her out here." She was going to lose her mind seeing him like this, but he didn't know who else to go to.

The cabbie nodded, and Jake handed him a folded bill. He stuffed it in his pocket as he hopped out of the car and headed for the tent. A few minutes later, he returned with Grace right behind him. She was still dressed in the red and gold uniform she wore for performances, and her mouth was set in a tight line.

The cabbie opened the door where Jake sat and pointed. "Right in here."

Grace bent to look inside, and Jake carefully swung his legs out onto the ground. When she got a good look at his face in the light, she put a hand over her mouth and gasped. "What happened?"

He pushed himself up, sending a new shock of pain up his spine. Everything spun. Unable to find his footing, he staggered forward. Grace was there to catch him. She put one of his arms over her shoulder and began leading him away, a gesture for which he was grateful. He doubted he could have made it very far on his own.

"Is he going to be all right?" the cabbie asked.

"I've got him, thanks." Her voice was high and shaky.

The boy got in his cab and drove away. Jake and Grace headed toward her tent, which was pitched a little closer to the animals.

"I'm fine," he said.

"You're *not* fine," she hissed. "What happened to you?"

"Burke."

"Burke did this?"

"And Clarence, and Sean, and some other mob thug I don't know."

"Why?" She held open the flap of her tent so he could duck under it, then helped him over to the cot.

He sat down with a groan and rubbed at his ribs. Considering how much it hurt to breathe, a few of them were probably cracked. "I gave Burke the money we've collected so far. Tried to make some kind of deal with him or convince him to give me more time. For a few minutes, it seemed like he was gonna work with me. Obviously, I was wrong." He tried to laugh, then winced from the pain that shot through his ribs and chest.

Grace's brows knit together in concern. She put a hand on his shoulder and gently pushed him back. "Here. Lie down, and I'll go find Miss Maria."

He grabbed her wrist. "No."

"You're a mess, Jake. You need a Healer."

"You're a Healer."

"Not a very good one."

"Good enough. Please, Grace, I don't want anyone else to know about this."

"They're going to know the second they see your face."

"Then I'll tell them I got in a fight. But not now. Not tonight. I don't wanna deal with anyone's questions."

She pursed her lips, then nodded. "Okay, then. I'll do the best I can."

He let go of her arm and laid his head on a pillow. Grace lit a lantern and went to the small cauldron hanging over a rock-lined pit in the center of the tent. She lit a fire underneath it and coaxed the flames to a steady blaze. After that, she pulled a bag out from under the cot and sat facing Jake while she searched its contents for the ingredients she needed. Her eyes narrowed in concentration as she read each label.

Jake drifted in and out of sleep as he watched her work. At one point, he woke to find that she'd removed his boots and draped a handknit blanket over him. Another time, he felt her dabbing at his face with a cool, wet cloth. Later, she woke him up to drink the potion she'd brewed, then knelt by the edge of the cot with her hands hovering over him as she muttered the spells to heal his injuries.

She started at his feet, then moved up his body one slow inch at a time, repeating a single phrase over and over again. Sweat glistened on her olive skin, then began to run down her face in drops from the effort. But it was working. Jake's pain subsided, never disappearing completely but reducing to a significantly more tolerable level.

When she got to his face, she ran her fingertips along his jaw, his nose, his eyes—anywhere there was a cut, a bruise, or swelling. He winced under her touch, but after a few minutes, the pain began to dissipate, and the swelling went down to the point that he could fully open both eyes again.

"That's better," he murmured. An electric pain still radiated from the site of his old back injury, but the rest of him felt almost new again.

Grace sat back and wiped at her face with her sleeve. "Once that potion wears off, some of the pain will probably return. But it shouldn't be as bad as before."

"Thank you."

"Sure."

Remorse weighed heavy in his chest as he watched her inhale deep breaths to recover from all the magic she'd used. She always looked strong, especially in her performance uniform, a woman as wild and powerful as the beasts she trained. Now, he only saw her fragility, how easily she could be broken. Burke's threat against her echoed inside his head like thunder warning of a coming storm.

"I'm sorry I got you involved in all this."

She shook her head, and her eyes burned with a bold fierceness he knew and loved. "Don't you dare apologize for that. I wanted to be involved. I want to help however I can. That's what you do when you love someone."

"Thank you."

"So, what are we going to do now?"

He eased himself up to a sitting position and shook his head. "I have no idea. I wish I could see a way out of this mess, but I can't. I've tried every damned thing I can think of, and—"

A new idea sprang into his mind as bright and vivid as a flash of lightning in the dark. A memory of an old man in a suit and a top hat. Words exchanged during a show. A business card trading hands. A name—Harvey Malone.

"What is it?" Grace asked.

"I just remembered something." He told her about the wealthy businessman who had approached him during a show a month ago. "I think he could be the solution to our problems."

"You still need more than two hundred thousand dollars, Jake. Do you really think he'd be willing to give us that much?"

"Not as an investment. But he might be willing to buy us out."

Her eyes widened. "You want to *sell* the circus? Are you crazy?"

"I don't *want* to, but I think I have to."

"Why not just sell it to Burke, then?" she said sarcastically. "That's what he wanted in the beginning, isn't it?"

She knew as well as he did that whatever the notorious mobster wanted with the circus couldn't be good. Selling it to him would be the ultimate last resort, and they weren't quite that desperate. Not yet.

"If we can convince Malone to buy the circus, we might be able to keep the show going. I've got seven more days to get

Burke the rest of his money. Six, after tonight. It's too late to do anything else, but this—Grace, this could work."

Her hands balled into fists in her lap. "You *can't* sell the circus. Cliff never would have been okay with it. These people, this show, it was everything to him."

"You don't think it is to me, too?"

The words caught him by surprise even as they tumbled out of his mouth. The circus had been an important part of his life for the past few years, but until now, he hadn't realized just how personally significant it had become. It was a part of him, and faced with the prospect of losing it, he felt the same way he had listening to one Healer after another tell him his career riding dragons was over. It was the same overwhelming storm of emotions, the most potent of which was frustration with how very little control he had over the circumstances that had led him here.

"I'm just scared," Grace said quietly. "Strickland's Circus is the only life I've ever known. What happens to all of us if the show's gone?"

Jake dragged himself out of his own melancholy and tried to see the brighter side of things. For her. Her entire world was crumbling, and she needed something to cling to. "Malone said this was the most incredible show he'd seen since he was a boy. I think he'll keep it going. Rename it after himself, maybe. Hire on some new acts, make a few other changes. But the circus itself would continue."

"And what about you?"

"What about me? I think I can convince Malone to let me stay on and work for him. Worst case scenario, I go find a job somewhere else. The point is, Burke gets his money, and I get to stay alive." And so would she.

She frowned. "I still don't like it, but it sounds like it's our only option."

"I'll go find that business card Malone gave me."

He started to stand up, but Grace was faster, and she put two hands on his shoulders to stop him. "Oh, no you won't.

Not now. You've had a very long, terrible day, and you need to rest. Malone can wait until morning."

Jake felt like there was an hourglass inside him, already draining sand faster than he could hope to keep up with, but Grace was right. Besides, it was late, and Malone was probably asleep. He laid back down and rolled onto his side to make space for her on the cot. She gently nestled herself into his arms, and within minutes, they were both asleep.

# CHAPTER 15

## LAST DITCH EFFORT

Grace was already gone when Jake woke up to pounding in his skull and an ache that seemed to radiate across his entire body, more intense in some places than others. He sat up carefully and went to rub the sleep out of his eyes, then winced as his fingers hit bruised skin. He needed to find a mirror, check out what the damage was before he went outside and ran into anyone else. Not that their stares and whispers would be avoidable, but he'd like to know exactly what they were staring at and whispering about.

The bag where Grace kept her potion ingredients was still sitting next to the small fire pit in the center of the tent. A corner of metal stuck out of the top, part of a small tray he'd seen her use for sorting and dividing ingredients. He pulled it out and held it up in front of him.

His face didn't look as bad as it felt, and he was sure it looked better than it had before Grace had done her healing. His left eye socket and cheekbone were still swollen and covered in a mass of deep purple bruises. Angry red cuts and scrapes smeared across that side of his face. The right side was a little better, with bruising just under the eye and dusting the bottom of his jaw. It definitely looked like he'd had a rough night, but he might be able to pass it off as a bar fight gone wrong instead of the brutal three-on-one beating he'd actually received.

He returned the tray to the bag, stood up, and stretched carefully. Judging by the light, it was late morning. It had been kind of Grace to let him rest, but now that he was up, it was time to contact Malone and hopefully put this whole mess behind him.

He combed his fingers through his hair, but it was difficult to tame the few clumps that still stuck up in odd places. He couldn't decide which was worse—his own dried blood or whatever other unknown substance he seemed to have picked up from his time spent sprawled in the alley gutter. Too bad he'd left his hat on the train yesterday; the wide brim would have helped to hide his hair and shield his face a little. But he had to go back to the train anyway to hunt down Malone's card. After pulling on his boots, he pushed the tent flap aside and stepped out.

Clarence stood at one of the corners, smoking a cigar. He gave a cordial nod as if the previous night's events had never happened. Rage seethed inside Jake at the memory of the ogre's fists smashing into his body over and over again, but there was nothing he could do to change it or make Clarence go away. Not until he got Burke his money.

"Getting a little extra beauty sleep this morning, are we?" Clarence taunted. "You definitely need it, though I must say you look better than you did the last time I saw you."

Jake strode past him without saying anything. The ogre followed, bringing the stench of his cigar along with him.

"Mr. Burke wanted me to remind you of your deadline. The money's still due in six days."

He clenched his jaw. "I'm aware."

"I hope you know how you're going to get the rest of it. As you've seen, the boss takes his business very seriously."

"Don't you have something better to do right now?"

"Sure, Jakey boy. Sure. Just wanted to make sure you got the message, that's all." He changed direction, whistling a cheerful tune as he headed off toward the menagerie.

Jake continued his walk to the trainyard. It was a little less than a mile away, and he spent the time rehearsing what he would say to Harvey Malone. He only had one shot to convince the man to buy the circus, and if that didn't work, he had no idea what he'd do next.

Once he reached the circus train, he stepped inside his sleeper car and looked around, trying to remember where he might have put Malone's business card the night they met. He rummaged through the crate that contained his father's old photo album and several other odds and ends, but it wasn't there. Next, he dug through the pockets of every pair of pants he owned, but he didn't find it there, either. He took out his billfold, wondering if the card had been on his person the whole time, but it wasn't.

Frantic thoughts began to run through his mind. What if he couldn't find the card? What if he'd lost his opportunity to get in touch with Mr. Malone? What if his own forgetfulness had doomed him?

He sat on the bed and tried to remember what he'd been doing that night after the show. It seemed so long ago, an entire lifetime away. He almost laughed at how carefree he'd been, even though he hadn't realized it then. Whatever financial troubles he'd thought he'd been struggling with at the time were nothing compared to what he was facing now.

He remembered doing some calculations by lantern light as the train left the city after the show. It was a routine task, but that particular night stood out because he'd been especially happy about ticket sales and how much higher they'd been compared to the year before. He knew because he had looked up the numbers and then recorded the difference in the route book.

The route book! He lifted the corner of the mattress where he kept the worn, leather-bound journal and pulled it out, then flipped through its pages with his thumb. The paper skipped irregularly toward the end. Stuck there against the binding was the cream-colored business card Malone had given him.

Jake pulled the card out and held it up for examination. The man's photo took up the entire front side. On the back, his name was printed in bold, black letters above a telephone number and an address in Ravington.

Relieved, Jake wedged the route book under his mattress and stuck the card in his pocket. He grabbed his hat from its hook on the wall, changed into some fresh clothes, and headed back to the circus lot. He needed to find Bruno.

That conversation was sure to be a delight. Bruno hadn't been willing to listen to his apologies the last time they'd spoken, but now, Jake needed him to. There were other Enchanters on the show who could facilitate communication with Malone, but none he could rely on like Bruno. He owed him another apology anyway, and at this point, he was willing to do whatever else it took to regain his friend's trust.

Bruno often spent his mornings in the performer's dressing tent trying to decide exactly what combination of nearly-identical pants, shirt, hat, and jacket he wanted to wear for the day's shows, so Jake headed straight there. As expected, he found the dwarf inside, adjusting the gold cuffs on a crimson jacket and then looking up to examine himself in the mirror.

He scowled when he caught sight of Jake in the reflection. "What happened to you?" Despite the stubborn gruffness in his tone, concern flickered in his eyes.

"It's nothing. Just a fight."

"With who, the townies? I didn't hear anything about a clem last night."

"No, it was in town. Bar fight."

"What were you doing at a bar in town?"

"It don't matter."

He grunted and went back to adjusting his suit. "More secrets then, is it? If you came looking for sympathy, you're in the wrong place."

Jake sighed. "Look, I can explain everything, but right now, I really need your help."

Bruno turned around to face Jake with his thick arms crossed over his chest. "Well, you'd better start with that explanation, then. You'll have to forgive me if I'm not inclined to just take you at your word anymore."

"Fine. But not here. Somewhere more discreet."

"There's nowhere more discreet. I can enchant the entrance, if you want. Make it impossible for anyone to come in here for a few minutes."

Jake nodded, and Bruno walked through the maze of costumes and props until he reached the tent flap. He muttered to himself and ran his fingertips along the entire thing before making his way back to Jake. "Well, come on then. Out with it."

"I don't know where to start."

"How about you start with what actually happened to you last night? Because that wasn't a bar fight, and it wasn't an accident, either. And that ogre who keeps following you around isn't your friend."

He'd put enough of the pieces together on his own that there was no point in trying to pretend anymore. Everything was falling apart, and Jake didn't want Bruno of all people blaming him for this or misunderstanding what he was trying to do. He sat down on a stepstool next to some crates full of colorful clown suits and told his friend everything. Even the part about Burke threatening Grace, which he'd intentionally withheld from her.

When he was finished, Bruno didn't say anything right away. His jaw worked up and down like he was chewing on something, trying to process everything Jake had said. At last, he simply grumbled, "You should have told me."

"It wouldn't have done any good, and I didn't wanna drag anyone else into it."

"You let us all hate you for downsizing the show."

"I figured I could work out a deal with Burke and set everything right again. If that meant people hated me for a little while, so be it."

Bruno shook his head. "You think they hated you then, just wait until they hear you're selling the show."

"I know. I don't like it either, but I'm hoping Malone will keep it going. At least through the end of the season. I could just give it over to the mob, but something tells me they're not all that interested in running an honest entertainment business."

"I guess we'd better contact this Mr. Malone, then." He took the card from Jake and went to stand beside the mirror. "You ready?"

Jake moved into position and straightened his shirt. "Ready."

Bruno touched his fingers to the mirror's surface. The reflection rippled, then came into focus to show an elderly man with wispy white hair and a perfectly trimmed mustache sitting in a swanky-looking office. He sat writing something with a fountain pen behind a polished desk, but he seemed to catch a glimpse of the shift in reflection and glanced in Jake's direction. He held up a finger as if asking him to wait just a moment, then finished whatever he was writing before standing up and coming closer.

"Jake Strickland. What a surprise. You look…forgive me, but you look awful. Are you all right?"

"I had a little accident, but I'm fine."

"I'm glad to hear that. What can I do for you?"

"Well, it's about the circus. There ain't no easy way to explain, so I'll just come out and say it. I'm in some financial trouble, and I need to sell the show. I remembered our conversation from that performance you came to, and I thought—I hoped—you might be interested."

Malone's big, round eyes blinked a few times behind his spectacles. "You want to sell Strickland's Circus?"

"I wouldn't say I want to, but I need the money. I don't really have any other choice."

Malone tilted his head to one side. "Financial trouble, you said?"

"Personal trouble, nothing to do with the business. The circus has been doing just fine. Ticket sales are good, crowds are still coming to see us, and we've seen a small but steady increase in profits throughout the season."

"Forgive me for asking, but if things are going so well, why would you sell your family business?"

"Like I said, I don't have any other options."

"Hmm. Well, it's certainly an interesting proposition. I have been looking for some creative investment opportunities, and circuses are incredibly popular these days. But to be perfectly honest, I'm not sure I'm the right man for the job. I don't know the first thing about running a circus."

Jake hadn't planned on bringing it up until later, but since Malone was asking, now seemed as good a time as any. "I'd be happy to stay on and teach you the ropes. Even if it's just to finish out the rest of the season. Not in my current capacity as owner, obviously, but maybe as some kind of manager or consultant."

"That's a kind offer." He glanced down at his watch. "I have a meeting to get to in a few minutes, but I'd love to discuss this further in person. Where's your show playing this weekend?"

"We're in Glassvale on Friday, then Haleston on Saturday and Pixie Point on Sunday."

"Perfect. I can be in Glassvale by Friday morning. I'll want to see your financial records, of course, and then we'll have to discuss price, but I'm sure we can come up with something that's fair to both of us."

Jake tried to temper his hopeful excitement before responding. "That sounds great. I'll see you on Friday."

"See you then. Goodbye."

Bruno touched the surface of the mirror, and the reflection returned to normal. "That went well."

"I just hope it works out," Jake replied. "If he won't buy the show…" He trailed off as a hundred possible unpleasant scenarios ran through his mind.

Bruno patted him on the arm. "He will. I'll make sure the others know to be on their best behavior when he comes. We'll give him the royal treatment, show him what a good investment this circus could be."

"Just don't say anything about the mob. They don't want anyone knowing they're involved, and I think it's best to keep them happy."

"I won't. And listen, Jake. The next time you find yourself in a mess like this, you tell me the truth to start with, all right? I can't promise I'll be able to do much to fix it, but I'd like the chance to try."

# CHAPTER 16

## HOPE FOR THE FUTURE

On Friday morning—just three days before Burke's deadline—a shiny car pulled up to the ticket office where Jake, Grace, and Bruno were waiting. The driver of the vehicle exited and held the back door open for a slight old man in a tailored three-piece suit. Harvey Malone approached Jake with an outstretched hand and an amicable smile peeping out from beneath his snow-white mustache.

"Hello again, Jake. It's good to see you."

He shook the man's hand. "Thank you for coming, Mr. Malone."

"Of course, of course. If nothing else, the opportunity to see your magnificent show again is quite the treat. And who are these fine people?"

"This is our master of ceremonies, Bruno Forgehelm. And Grace Hawkins, who trains the griffins and our dragon."

Malone's eyes brightened. "Ah, yes, of course. I thought you looked familiar. That act was one of my favorites!"

Grace gave him a little curtsy. "Thank you."

"They've both been on the show a lot longer than I have," Jake went on, "so I asked them to join us on the tour to answer any questions you might have."

"A tour! Oh, how delightful. A rare opportunity to peer behind the curtain and get a look at what makes this place so magical."

Jake smiled. The man was clearly enamored with the circus already. How hard could it be to convince him purchasing it would be a smart business move?

They started their walk around the circus lot. Bruno was a natural tour guide, and Jake let him and Grace do most of the talking. They explained each part of the circus and told charming anecdotes about its tradition and history. Malone ate up every word like a kid with a bag full of cotton candy.

The group spent a full hour in the menagerie before it was opened up to the townies who'd purchased tickets. Here and there throughout the tour, they stopped to meet some of the performers. Everyone was gracious and welcoming, treating Malone like he was visiting royalty and not some stranger come to snatch up their show. Bruno was probably to thank for that, for which Jake was grateful.

They saved the ring stock tent for last. Malone's face lit up in childish delight when he walked past all the performing animals. Grace coaxed Trigger and Bullseye out of their corner so Malone could pet them, but the true star, as usual, was Calico Thunder. Malone watched in amazement while Grace walked the dragon through a few of her more low-key tricks, which included standing up on her hind legs and extending one clawed foreleg to shake Jake's hand. She lowered her chest and forelegs to the ground in a sort of bow when she was done, then stretched out on the dirt and yawned.

Malone applauded her performance. "Bravo! What a magnificent creature, and certainly a unique part of your collection. You don't see many dragons in circuses these days."

"They can be expensive to feed and transport," Jake said. "But she's smaller than most, so that helps. We think she's worth the cost. She's definitely a crowd favorite."

“I can see why. She’s quite a charmer.” Malone smiled at the dragon like she was a puppy in a pet shop window, and Jake’s lingering misgivings about selling the show to the polished businessman dissipated.

He clearly loved the circus. For him, it wasn’t just an easy way to make a profit. He seemed to understand its splendor and magic, and from what Jake could tell, he loved the animals most of all. That was more than Jake could have hoped for. He still wasn’t thrilled about having to give up the show, but there were worse people he could sell to than Harvey Malone, and Malone was definitely a better choice than Vincent Burke.

“Well, then,” Malone said, “I think I’ve seen all I need to here. Thank you for the lovely tour, Ms. Hawkins, Mr. Forgehelm.” He shook each of their hands before turning to Jake. “Do you happen to have those financial records I asked about?”

“They’re in the office, over by the ticket booth.”

“Good. Let’s take a look at them, shall we?”

Grace and Bruno went their own way, and Jake led Malone to the brightly painted red wagon that served as the show’s administrative office. He unlocked the door and motioned for the man to have a seat in one of the chairs at a small table, then went to a chest that sat in the corner. He flipped through the files inside until he found the ones he needed and took them to the table, where he sat across from Malone.

They spent the next two hours combing through the show’s financial records, examining each month’s expenditures and profits going back five years. Malone asked Jake several questions throughout the process, particularly about the time period two seasons ago when his father had died and he’d taken over as the show’s owner. Jake answered the questions with complete transparency, never going so far as to disparage his father, but still making it clear that Cliff had been an irresponsible businessman.

When Malone looked at all those negative numbers listed under monthly profits, Jake needed him to see that the circus itself had never been the problem. Now that Cliff wasn't around to make erratic decisions based in fantasy rather than reality, the show was doing just fine.

After reviewing everything thoroughly, Malone leaned back in his chair. He took off his spectacles and cleaned them with a silk handkerchief from his pocket. "From everything I can see, this looks like a solid investment. Let's talk about price."

Not wanting to appear too eager, Jake forced himself to take a moment before answering. He still had to get enough money out of this sale to pay off the rest of his debt, after all. "If I had a little more time to find a buyer, I'd probably ask at least three hundred and fifty thousand dollars for it all. Given the circumstances, I'm willing to take three hundred."

Malone stroked his mustache while he considered the offer. "Three hundred still seems a bit steep. Would you take two seventy?"

Jake had been expecting that. He tilted his head to the side and crossed his arms, considering Malone's offer. It was enough, but he still had one last card to play, and he had to at least give it a shot. "I'll do two seventy if you can promise you'll keep everyone on for the rest of the season."

"I don't see any problem with that. You have a deal." He stuck his hand across the table to seal the agreement.

As Jake clasped the man's palm, relief enveloped him like a warm blanket. He didn't have the money yet, but barring some freak accident or cruel act of God, he was free. Burke would get his money, Jake would keep his life, and Grace wouldn't be in any danger of the mob's threats. Not only that, but he'd managed to save everyone's jobs in the process, and he'd end up with enough extra money to pay them a good portion of the wages he'd been forced to hold back.

The relief passed, and a profound sense of emptiness followed in its wake. Jake had only felt something similar once before, when the truth of his career-ending injury really sank in for the first time. He'd poured every ounce of energy he had into this circus over the past two years. He'd never asked for the responsibility, but he'd been good at running things. Somewhere along the way, he'd even come to love it. The circus was his family, his life, his future. Priceless.

And he'd just sold it for two hundred and seventy thousand dollars.

"Would you like me to write you a check?" Malone said, already reaching inside his jacket for his checkbook.

Jake pulled himself out of his wallowing to consider the question. "Cash would be better, even if it takes a couple days."

The man gave him a curious look but didn't question his decision. "Cash it is, then. I'll have it to you by Monday morning."

Monday was the same day he was supposed to pay Burke. It was cutting things close, and there would be no room for anything to go wrong with the bank or transportation or anything else involved in getting the money from Malone to Jake and then to Burke. "The sooner the better."

Malone stood up from the table. He straightened his suit jacket and headed for the door. "I'll have my lawyer draw up all the paperwork. I can send someone with it tomorrow for you to look over, and we can sign it on Monday when I bring the money. Does that sound fair?"

Jake hurried to open the door for the older man. "Absolutely. Thank you so much, Mr. Malone. I really appreciate it."

"Thank *you*. And don't think I've forgotten about your offer to stay on to help with the transition after the sale is finalized. I assume you'll still need a job?"

"I'd very much appreciate that, sir."

"Good." Malone tipped his hat and shook Jake's hand one last time before heading out the door. "It's been a pleasure, Mr. Strickland. I look forward to working with you in the future."

♦ ♦ ♦

That night, Jake waited until Clarence was sleeping to go find Grace. He had a surprise waiting for her in the train car Calico Thunder shared with Trigger and Bullseye. Nothing too fancy, but he'd put some forethought into it, and the look of surprise on her face when she stepped inside was more than enough reward to make his efforts worthwhile.

Several mismatched lanterns hung from the ceiling. The glass encasing them had been temporarily colored by Bruno's enchantments to illuminate the car in soft, pastel colors. At Jake's request, Otto had stowed the fairy box next to the griffins' enclosure rather than in one of the menagerie cars, and the tiny creatures' frolicking splashed dancing spots of brighter light against every surface. A heavy quilt lay spread out on the floor in front of the fairy box, and wildflowers Jake had picked that evening sat on a picnic basket in the center.

Grace turned to him with a playful smile and draped her arms over his shoulders. "Now what's all this about, cowboy?"

"I wanted to thank you."

She quirked an eyebrow. "Is that so? For what, exactly?"

Where to even begin? "For everything. You've been so supportive, and I want you to know how much I appreciate that. I'm sure it hasn't been easy on you, but I couldn't have handled any of this on my own. So thank you."

She kissed him, then pulled away slightly to whisper against his lips. "Well, we both know you'd be helpless without me."

He laughed. "Come on. Let's eat something."

"There's food, too? You really do know the way to a girl's heart."

He led her to the blanket and began unpacking the picnic basket. The cooks had been kind enough to give him some of the leftovers from that night's dinner, which he'd used to make sandwiches. He'd also bought a bag of kettle corn from concessions before they left. Grace always said she'd eaten too much of the stuff as a kid and wouldn't buy it for herself, but she seemed to love it anyway. She opened up the bag and put a few pieces in her mouth before even looking at her sandwich.

"Pretty lights." Her eyes slowly scanned the rest of the train car. "You get Bruno to do them for you?"

"Yeah."

"He was great with Malone today, wasn't he? A natural tour guide."

"A natural showman," Jake said. "Thrives on any chance he gets to show off a little. But you were both great. Taking Malone around like that and telling him about all the great things the circus has to offer—that was what really sealed the deal."

"I'm glad we could help." They ate in silence for a few minutes before she said anything else. "Do you think he'll be okay? As a boss, I mean. Running this place."

"It don't really matter what I think anymore. What do you think?"

"He seems nice. It's just hard to imagine this place being owned and operated by someone else. I mean, it *is* Strickland's Circus."

"That's just a name."

"A name that belongs to two of the best men I've ever known."

Under other circumstances, he might have been annoyed that anyone put him in the same category as his father. But this was Grace, and she'd just called him one of the best men she knew. His chest swelled with warmth and pride. "I'll still be around, you know. It's not my circus anymore, but I'll still be managing things."

"For now," Grace said, her voice soft and tinged with sadness. She broke off pieces of the chicken in her sandwich and tossed them through the wood slats to Trigger and Bullseye. "What happens after the end of the season?"

Jake's heartrate sped up, and the corners of the cube-shaped object in his pocket seemed to dig into his leg. He wanted to say something, but his mouth suddenly felt dry and pinched.

Grace went on. "It's just, everyone leaves, you know? First my mom, then my dad. Then Cliff. Now you." She threw the last piece of her sandwich to the griffins and wrung her hands in her lap. "I've always prided myself on being strong and able to take care of myself. But the truth is, I don't want to be alone. I don't want anyone else to leave."

"I ain't going nowhere."

"Not yet."

She was worrying about things that hadn't even happened yet, things that might not happen at all. He wished he could solve everything simply by telling her she didn't need to worry, but where he was practical, she was emotional, always looking at a dozen potential what-ifs instead of what was already right in front of her. Maybe that made her smarter than him, all that thinking about the future. In fact, it almost certainly did. But Jake could only work with *now*.

And right now, he had something he needed to tell her. Something he'd been wanting to tell her for a long time. He pulled the small box out of his pocket and held it discreetly under one palm as he took her hand in the other.

"I ain't leaving, Grace. I mean it. I've never had much of a problem with being alone, but I don't wanna be alone without you. I love you."

"I love you, too, but—" She gave him a quizzical look as he pushed himself up off the ground. "What are you doing?"

He knelt on one knee in front of her and opened the box that held his grandmother's ring. His heart was racing, and the air suddenly felt much too warm, but his voice came out strong and steady as he looked her in the eyes. "I just sold everything I own. I'm broke, and I have no idea what kind of life I can offer you in the future—not that you ever needed anyone to take care of you. But I wanna try, and if you'll have me, I promise to love you 'til the day I die. Marry me, Grace. Please."

She moved closer to him, and a slow smile spread across her face. Fairy lights glittered in her eyes like stars as she nodded. "Of course I'll marry you, cowboy. It took you long enough to ask."

All his pent-up anxiety and emotion came rolling out in a deep, long laugh. Grace laughed, too, and they were still giggling like two mischievous schoolkids as he slipped the ring over her finger. She admired it in the colored lights for a few seconds, and Jake sat back down. He put his arm around her shoulders as she snuggled up against him.

He had lost so much today, but he didn't care. For the first time in almost a month, all he could feel was joy. He had Grace, and she had chosen him, and right now, here in the night in their sheltered sanctuary, nothing else mattered.

# CHAPTER 17

## THE MOBSTER'S RETURN

Monday morning dawned bright and clear, a perfect day with a pure blue sky overhead. The circus was in Ravington, one of the largest cities on the eastern side of the country and—conveniently—Harvey Malone's hometown. According to Jake's watch, it was 7:45 a.m. Malone had said he'd be here first thing in the morning with the money, and that was what he was counting on as he stood near the ticket booth to wait. He just hoped Burke didn't show up first.

Beside him, Clarence stood with his hands in his pockets and whistled a cheerful tune. He'd said almost nothing to Jake since the morning after the alley incident, but just being in the ogre's presence made him seethe. Visions of retribution flashed through his mind. He always came out of these imagined fights victorious and unscathed, but he didn't delude himself that it would play out that way in real life.

A sleek, four-door touring car rolled up. Finally. Jake took a step forward but froze when he saw the vehicle's occupants through the window. The front doors opened, and it wasn't Harvey Malone and his driver who stepped out. It was Burke and Sean.

Burke ginned and approached the ticket booth, a briefcase swinging in one hand. What was inside it? A machine gun, maybe, or a few pistols. Maybe even a bomb. Some tool to end Jake and his circus once Burke learned he didn't have the money.

How was he going to talk himself out of this? His mind raced but couldn't seem to settle on anything useful. He'd made the mistake of thinking Burke could be reasonable before, but now he knew better. He needed that money.

Where the hell was Malone?

Burke stopped in front of him. "Good morning, Jake."

He shook the mobster's hand and tried not to grimace. It was like reaching out to pick up a snake. "Good morning."

"You look a little pale. Are you sick? Or maybe just feeling a bit ill at ease?"

"I'm fine." His throat felt like sandpaper. He wracked his brain again for something to say, some way to begin this conversation so he wouldn't just piss Burke off. But all the intelligence and good sense he'd ever had seemed to have abandoned him. He couldn't come up with a single thing.

"Well, I'm sure you know why I'm here," Burke said. "But first, we have some other business to take care of." He raised the briefcase to his chest and tapped a single finger against its surface. "Harvey Malone asked me to bring this to you."

*Harvey Malone?* Jake's thoughts went spinning even faster. "What is it?"

"It's your money, of course. From the circus sale. Though, since you'll just be giving most of it back to me, I think I'll hold onto it." He glanced over his shoulder at Sean and snapped his fingers. The ogre held out his arms. Burke laid the briefcase across them and opened it up. Stacks of bills lined the interior—more money than Jake had ever seen in his life and probably more than he would ever see again.

Burke ran a hand over the top layer of cash. "Adding what you already gave me to what's in here, it seems twenty-five thousand dollars of this is yours. Malone contributed that himself. Very gentlemanly of him. I can't say I would have done the same, but I think he felt bad about his part in all this. Not that he ever had much choice."

Another question floated to the surface of Jake's jumbled thoughts. "You know Malone?"

"Of course I know Harvey. Who do you think set this all up in the first place?"

He turned back to Jake with a stack of cash in his hand. Except now, it wasn't the face and body of a grown man that greeted him. It was a boy. A boy of about ten years old, with dark hair, rosy cheeks, and Burke's familiar, unnaturally wide smile.

The same boy who had been with Malone that first night he and Jake met under the big top.

His stomach went hollow. "You set me up."

Burke sighed. "Yes, that's what I just said." The glamour he'd been using to disguise his appearance vanished, and he was a grown man once more.

Jake's hands curled into tight fists. "Did my father even owe you all that money, or was that a lie, too?"

Burke scowled. "Now that's uncalled for. I've been perfectly fair and honest with you and your father, which is more than I can say for him. I admit I hid my true identity when we first met, but that was only because I needed to introduce you to Harvey without revealing my involvement."

Why, though? Why had he gone to all the trouble of organizing this scheme with Malone in the first place instead of just leaving Jake to come up with the money himself?

Unless the money had never been what they were really after.

A cold chill squeezed his chest and spread through his veins like icy water. Burke had wanted the circus from the very first day he'd shown up. He'd offered to forgive Cliff's debts if Jake turned over the show. And Clarence had tried to keep him from buying that luck charm, which only made sense if he didn't actually want Jake to have any success selling the animals and equipment. But why?

"What do you want with the circus?" he asked.

"That's none of your concern anymore."

"You're right. But it is Mr. Malone's. We signed a contract. You can't just—"

Burke clicked his tongue and shook his head. "You really should have had a lawyer look that over. It wasn't even real."

Jake opened his mouth to say something else, but no words came. There was nothing to say. They'd played him. The game had been rigged from the start.

Burke laid a hand on his shoulder. "Don't look so gloomy. This way, everyone wins. You walk away with all your limbs still attached to your body, and we get the circus. By the time we sell the tent, the wagons, and whatever other useless garbage you keep lying around, we'll make a nice little profit. But the animals are where the real money's at."

"What do you mean?"

He shrugged one shoulder. "Business is booming, thanks to the Ban. People are buying even more charms and jinxes now than they were before it was illegal. We can barely keep up, partly because the ingredients are so hard to come by. Basilisk venom, cockatrice blood, phoenix and griffin feathers—it's all in very high demand. I could get a hundred grand just from that dragon you've got, once she's been taken apart. Her hide alone would be worth fifty thousand to the right buyer. Honestly, I'm surprised you didn't think of it yourself."

Jake lunged at Burke, even as the more logical part of his mind warned him against doing anything stupid. He punched him right in the mouth, eager to obliterate that big, toothy grin of his. A mistake, since Clarence grabbed him by his suspenders and threw him to the ground a second later. But *damn*, it felt good.

Sean towered over him and drew back his foot for a kick, but Burke called out before he could do anything. “That’s enough, Sean.”

The ogre backed away, and Jake stood up to brush himself off. Pain radiated from his left side into his lower back, but seeing the spots of blood on Burke’s handkerchief as he dabbed at his mouth made it all worthwhile.

“You should go,” he growled.

“You’re right. I have other business to attend to, but Clarence will be staying behind to monitor the transition. You’ll stay, too. I want you somewhere we can keep an eye on you until this whole thing is over. Make up whatever excuses you want when you tell your crew, but it’s probably best for everyone if you don’t mention our involvement. If I can’t trust you to keep your mouth shut, well....” He shrugged. “I’m sure I don’t need to remind you what happened in Griffinsburg?”

Jake shook his head.

“Finish your performances tonight, but all your people need to be out of here by dawn.”

They had even less time than Jake had expected. That hook to Burke’s jaw had lost him whatever leverage he might have had to ask for favors, but he’d be doing a disservice to his people if he didn’t say anything. “You’ve gotta give us more time than that. This is their home. They ain’t got nowhere else to go.”

“That’s not my problem.”

At this point, he wasn’t above begging. “Please. This is gonna be hard enough on them already.”

Burke’s eyes narrowed. After a few seconds, he let out an exaggerated huff. “Fine. Tomorrow evening, then. But it’s your responsibility to keep them out of the way. I’ll have men coming to collect everything, and I don’t want any trouble. I think we’ve all had enough of that already.”

“Of course. No trouble.”

"Good." He returned his blood-spotted handkerchief to his pocket. "I'd say it's been a pleasure doing business with you, but I don't think that would be true for either of us. Here's hoping we never run into each other again."

Jake couldn't agree more. He spat on the ground and glared at Burke's back as the mobster returned to his car.

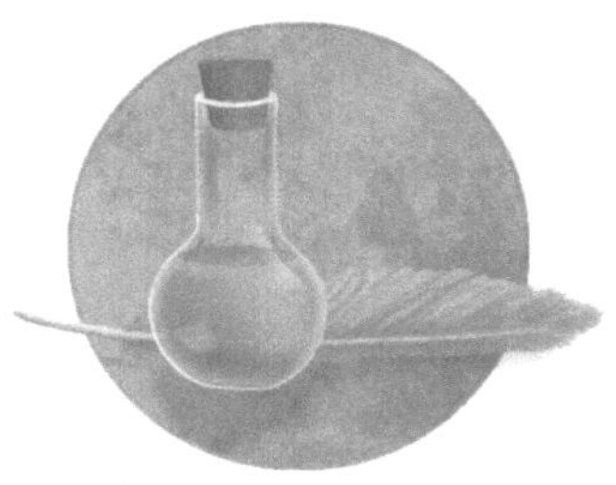

# CHAPTER 18

## SURVIVAL INSTINCT

If he'd had the choice, Jake wouldn't have broken the news to the others about the show's demise until after their final performance. Let them have one more good night under the big top doing what they loved, one more show that wasn't overshadowed by frustration and malcontent.

But that wasn't a choice he had. The roustabouts always packed up the menagerie and other nonessential parts of the circus as soon as the second show of the night began. Tonight, it all needed to stay where it was so Burke's men could start collecting everything in the morning. He had to tell them.

He gathered everyone together in the center ring under the big top to make the announcement. Townies were already lined up outside waiting to take their seats, but they could wait a few minutes longer. He stood atop one of the round pedestals used in the elephant act with Clarence on the ground behind him. The ogre had been stuck to him like a magnet ever since Burke left, and Jake hadn't had a chance to talk to Grace or Bruno or anyone else about the morning's events. They'd hear the bad news the same way everyone else would, off-guard and out-of-the-blue.

He looked around at the curious faces of the troupers before him. Since Malone's visit, rumors had spread that the show might have a change in owners, but thanks to Bruno's reassurances, no one had seemed too concerned about losing their jobs.

All of that was about to change.

He cleared his throat and waited for them to quiet down before speaking. "Thank you all for coming. I'm sorry to pull you away from your preparations, but I've got something important to say that couldn't wait."

A whisper rippled through their ranks. Jake waited a few seconds, took a breath, and kept going. "There have been rumors going around about the show being sold to the gentleman who came here last week. Many of you met him. Those rumors are true, but...well, I'm afraid the news is a lot worse than that."

He found Grace's face in the crowd and faltered. She stared back at him with confusion in her eyes and a questioning tilt of her head. This wasn't the way he'd wanted her to find out.

"Come on, lad," Otto shouted from the back of the crowd. "Out with it!"

Jake delivered the words he'd rehearsed with a stiff formality. "The new owner has decided to take things in a new direction. Unfortunately, that means none of us will be able to keep our jobs. Effective immediately."

There were a few seconds of stunned silence before a rumbling murmur began to spread. Grace looked even more confused than before. She nodded absently to the acrobat trying to talk to her and twisted the ring around her finger, all the while maintaining direct eye contact with Jake. He wished he could explain more, but for their own good, the others couldn't know about the mob's involvement in any of this. Burke had made that very clear. He'd have to find another time to talk to her privately.

Their voices grew louder, and before long, most of them were shouting at him.

"You can't do this!"

"Where are we supposed to go now?"

"You lied to us!"

Jake raised his hands in a futile attempt to quiet them. "I'm sorry. This ain't what I wanted either, but I didn't have any other choice. Please trust me on that."

"Trust you?" a clown in the front shouted. "You haven't even paid us what we've already earned. How do you expect us to survive out there with nothing?"

"I'm gonna pay you. I have enough to pay most of what I owe you. Not all of it, which I know ain't fair. But it's something."

That seemed to calm them a little. The angry roar reduced to a milder collective muttering, and although they still regarded Jake with anger and frustration, there was a little less hatred in their eyes. It was the best he was going to get.

"I'm sorry," he said again. "You all deserve better. I wish I could explain more, but I can't. All I can ask is that you believe me when I say I did everything I could to prevent this. We still have two more shows to do, and I know I shouldn't be asking you to perform after what I just told you, but I'm asking anyway. Everything we earn today goes toward your wages. I'll pay everyone in the morning, but the new owner wants us gone by tomorrow night. Take your personal belongings, but everything else should stay where it is. People will be coming by tomorrow to pack things up and move them off the lot."

The performers conversed amongst themselves for a few minutes. Jake couldn't hear everything, but the bits and pieces he picked up indicated they were debating whether they should go along with his request.

Bruno's baritone voice rose over the rest. "If this is going to be our last performance together, I say we make sure these townies remember Strickland's Circus as the most fantastic show any of them have ever seen."

The hum of conversation resumed, but now it was laced with unity rather than hostility and agreement rather than dissent. Grace squeezed between bodies to make her way to where Jake stood.

She climbed up onto the pedestal beside him and called out to the others. “Well come on, then. What are we waiting for? We’ve got a show to put on.”

A few people clapped or let out whoops of agreement and headed off to finish preparing for the show. Grace pivoted to face Jake. There wasn’t much room on the pedestal for both of them, and they stood so close their toes were touching. “What happened?” she hissed.

He wanted nothing more than to tell her, but he couldn’t let Clarence think they were plotting anything. “Not now.”

“Jake—”

He flicked his gaze over his shoulder to where the ogre stood. “Not now.”

Her eyes narrowed, but she seemed to understand and gave him a slight nod. “Meet me out back during the spec.”

Before he could respond, she hopped off the pedestal and slipped away with the others. Jake waited a few seconds before stepping down himself. He headed for the entrance to start letting the audience in.

Clarence fell into stride beside him. “That was inspiring.”

Jake gave him a cold stare. He wasn’t in the mood for sarcasm.

“No, I mean that. Not everyone can tell an entire group of people they’re fired and then convince them to work another day anyway.”

There was nothing inspiring about it. If anything, it was manipulative. They were performers. Many of them would have performed for free as long as there was someone to watch them.

He turned back to examine the big top, now empty aside from a few workers charged with keeping the show running smoothly. There was something calming about the place in the moments right before a show. Even with the chatter of the crowd and the shrieks of excited children just outside, in here, it was peaceful, almost reverent. He'd often taken that for granted, but now that everything was slipping away, he realized it was one of the things he was going to miss most.

He took in the silence for a moment longer, then nodded to the woman standing at the entrance. She opened the tent to take tickets and let the townies inside.

Jake stood back as they filed past. Clarence stood with him for a few minutes but soon lost interest. "I'm going to go find a good seat," he said. "Don't go anywhere too far."

He lumbered away, leaving Jake alone to watch the stands fill up and listen to the growing anticipation of the crowd.

He stood there for more than half an hour, until Bruno stepped into the ring in his elegant red-and-gold ensemble, complete with the lavishly-embellished top hat he typically reserved for special occasions. The crowd cheered, eager for the show to start, and he welcomed them all with his usual theatrical animation. Then the spec began, and as the band struck up a marching tune, performers and animals alike filed into the big top to make their way around the hippodrome track.

Trigger and Bullseye pranced side by side at the front of the procession with Calico Thunder just behind them, but it was Otto who led them, not Grace. Jake waited for an opportunity to escape Clarence's watchful eye so he could go meet her. When the elephants passed by, he ducked between a pair of them and slipped out of the big top.

She was waiting for him outside at the back of the tent. When he was within reach, she grabbed his hand and led him to the dressing tents. There was no one inside, and he followed her into the midst of haphazardly-hung clothes on racks that normally held the performers' costumes.

"What happened?" she asked. "I thought you gave Burke his money."

He quickly explained everything, and Grace's expression shifted from curiosity to dismay to rage. "Malone was just one of their pawns, too. That slimy, rotten piece of—"

"I don't think he had much choice. It sounded like Burke was manipulating him, too."

She waved a hand dismissively. "What's our next move, then?"

He shook his head in confusion. "What?"

"We're not just going to sit here and let them sell the animals for parts. So, what do we do next?"

"There's nothing left to do. We're out of moves here."

She crossed her arms. "No. We're not quitting. The Jake Strickland I know is not a man who rolls over in the dirt and gives up when things get tough."

Had she not seen everything he'd been doing for the past month trying to fix this whole mess? "I ain't giving up. I'm trying to survive. I'm trying to avoid any more trouble with the mob so we can all make it out of this in one piece."

"All of us except the animals, you mean."

"Grace, they're not gonna kill the animals." At least, not most of them.

"Oh, right. They're just going to take everything they can use from them. Rip the pieces they want off them and torture them until they die."

"That's not—"

"What about Calico Thunder? Burke told you they're going to skin her and sell her hide. Are you really going to sit by and let that happen?"

"Better her than the rest of us."

Her jaw dropped, and the fury in her eyes blazed even brighter. "I can't believe you would say something like that."

"What do you want me to say? I don't like it any more than you do, but this ain't just some petty crook we're dealing with. It's the Viterian mob. They almost killed me, and I don't plan on giving them an excuse to try again." He lowered his voice and shook his head. "They threatened to kill you, too. I can't let that happen. So what do you want me to do, Grace? What is it you expect from me?"

Her eyes welled up, but the tears never fell. She clamped her mouth shut and stared at him a few seconds longer, then walked past him without saying anything.

He reached out for her hand. "Grace, wait."

She pulled away. "I should get ready for my act."

He stood where he was and watched her go, wishing he knew what to say or do that might make this just a little easier on her.

# CHAPTER 19

## UNRAVELING

The cookhouse lacked its usual animated breakfast chatter the next morning, and all eyes turned to Jake as he dragged one of the tables out into the sun. He sat behind it the same way he had every payday for the past two years. Normally, a line had already formed before he even got set up, but now, not a single person came over.

It was almost like they were reluctant to admit the show was really over. Some of them had been with Strickland's Circus for longer than Jake had been alive. For Grace, Bruno, Otto, and others like them, it was the only life they really knew.

And now it was gone. Snuffed out before they even had a chance to register what was happening.

He instinctively looked for Grace among them, and a new pang of guilt stabbed at his chest when he couldn't find her. They hadn't seen each other since last night, and he'd opted to give her some space while he attended to other matters. It was selfish, but a part of him wished she was here now just to give him some moral support.

He'd been up all night dividing everything he had left and sorting the money into envelopes. In the end, the calculations had come out better than he'd expected. He'd kept just forty dollars for himself, enough to buy a couple train tickets and a few decent meals on the way to wherever Grace decided she wanted to go. He'd follow her anywhere, assuming she would still have him. It was the only certainty he had for the future, but it was enough.

Bruno was the first to approach. He carried his chair under one arm and shook his head when Jake reached into the wooden crate for his check. "You look like you could use some company." He came around to the other side of the table and set his chair beside Jake's.

"Thanks."

"Grace told me everything. I'm sorry things didn't work out like you planned."

"I'm sorry, too."

"Nothing to be sorry about. But I think the others would understand a whole lot better if they knew the truth. It might make things easier on them. And on you." He spoke in a hushed tone and nodded to Clarence eating at a table several yards away. "We could spread the word quietly. The ogre never has to know."

It was a tempting proposition, and the truth would certainly make things easier on everyone. But that was only a short-term solution, if it could be called a solution at all. News like that was prone to spreading beyond the confines of its intended audience, and Burke clearly didn't want anyone finding out what had really happened here. Maybe because he didn't want to attract any special attention from law enforcement, or maybe because he didn't want rival criminal organizations catching on to his scheme and replicating it to increase their own wealth and influence. Who knew what lengths the mobster would be willing to go to to keep things quiet? Already, two more people knew the truth than were supposed to.

He shook his head. "We can't tell anyone else. It's for their own good."

Bruno's eyebrows furrowed, but he nodded. "All right, then. If that's how you want it."

A small group of roustabouts tentatively approached the table. They were all young, teenagers or barely older, and they pushed and jostled each other as they whispered an argument. It seemed no one wanted to be the first in line.

Finally, the shortest, youngest-looking one stepped forward. He planted both feet in front of Jake and looked him square in the eye. There was some kind of challenge in his expression, but whatever it was about, Jake couldn't be sure. Maybe he was just pissed about losing his job, like everyone else, though he barely looked old enough to have a job in the first place.

"Name?" he asked.

"Edward Evans."

Bruno searched the crate for the envelope marked with the name while Jake ran a finger down his list until he found it. Wages in hand, the boy stepped aside to wait for his friends.

More people were lining up now. Before long, Jake and Bruno could hardly pass out the money fast enough. It was a good thing—the sooner they all left, the better—but he couldn't help feeling like everything was suddenly unraveling faster than he could keep up.

They were still handing out envelopes when Burke's men began to arrive on the lot. At first, there were only a handful of them. When Jake looked up again a few minutes later, there were dozens. They immediately set to work tearing down tents, packing animals into cages, and loading them into trucks and wagons, either their own or those that had once belonged to the circus. As Bruno handed out the last few envelopes, a caravan of them drove away in a cloud of dust.

The line in front of the table reached its end, and when Jake looked up, most of the familiar faces he'd come to know so well over the past few years were gone. Those that remained wandered aimlessly, watching Burke's men pick everything apart like vultures stripping a carcass. Clarence watched, too, whistling happily in between puffs of his cigar.

There were still two envelopes lying in the crate. Bruno stood up and pulled them both out. One belonged to him, and he pocketed it with a sad, nostalgic sort of look in his eyes. The other one had Grace's name scrawled across the front, and he handed it to Jake. "Well, I suppose that's it, then."

"Where will you go?" Jake asked.

Bruno shrugged. "There's always work in town for an Enchanter. I can do that for now, maybe try to join up with another show next season."

"Any show would be lucky to have you." An awkward silence hung in the air between them for a moment. Jake had never been very good at goodbyes, but he stood up and stuck his hand out to his friend. "Well, take care of yourself."

Bruno shook his hand, but his amethyst eyes twinkled. "Oh, I'm not leaving just yet. Not until they force me to. And don't you dare think about going anywhere without saying goodbye first."

"I wouldn't—"

A loud cry cut him off, and he was out of his seat and running toward the sound before he even fully registered what he was doing. But that was Grace's voice. He had to get to her. Now.

Another shout pierced the air, this time accompanied by an animal's shriek. The stock tents. He altered his course and urged more speed from his legs.

When he arrived, panting, Grace was fighting with two of Burke's men. Each one held a lead rope attached to Trigger and Bullseye's halters.

"You can't take them! Leave them alone!" She raised her fists and attempted to bring them down on the man leading Bullseye, but his partner reached out in time to block her blows.

"Get out of here! They're not yours anymore."

"They'll always be mine. You can't have them."

Sensing their mistress' distress, both griffins screeched frantically and fought their handlers. They pulled against the ropes with all their strength and reared up on powerful leonine legs. Trigger spread his wings as if to fly, nearly knocking down both men in the process.

Grace seized the opportunity and attempted to rip the rope away from the man holding Trigger. He backhanded her across the face, and she stumbled.

Jake sprinted at the man with every intention of launching himself into him. Before he got close enough, the man dropped his rope and pulled out the revolver on his hip.

Jake skidded to a stop beside Grace and sidestepped in front of her. The man leveled his gun at both of them, but it wasn't enough to stop Grace from trying to get to her griffins. She pushed past Jake. He grabbed her arm and held her fast as she attempted to wrench free.

The man pulled back the hammer on his revolver. "Take one more step, circus freak. Try me."

Grace's entire body trembled, but knowing her, it was from rage rather than fear. For a moment, she stopped fighting, and Jake relaxed his grip around her wrist. "Please, Grace," he said softly. "Just—"

"No!" She tore away from him and charged ahead.

The man turned around and grabbed one of the two ropes his companion now held. With a yank, he forced Trigger's head down and pressed the barrel of the gun to his skull.

Grace froze in place. "No, please." Her voice shook. "Please don't. You can't."

"I can do whatever I damn well please," the man growled.

Trigger and Bullseye continued to pull at their ropes, but now that no one else was shouting, they weren't putting up much of a fight. Jake wanted to be next to Grace, wanted to reach out and take her hand, but he didn't dare move. Not while there was a gun aimed at Trigger's head.

The man glared at Grace through narrowed eyes. "These beasts are worth more alive than they are dead, but it's not enough of a difference that I'll feel bad killing them right here if I have to. Anything to save us the trouble of your theatrics."

"I'm sorry, all right?" Her voice hitched on a sob. "I'm sorry. Please. Just put the gun away."

"I don't think so. We need to get these animals into that wagon, and you're going to help us. Calmly, and without any more disruptions. Do you understand?"

She nodded and took slow steps forward to meet her griffins. A whimper escaped her lips as she stroked their feathers with shaking hands. "It's okay, my handsome boys. Shh. There you are, everything's all right."

The man stepped back and allowed her to take Trigger's rope, but he kept his revolver up. Jake slowly walked over to take Bullseye from the second man. Together, he and Grace led the animals toward the wagon with Burke's men flanking them. The gun stayed trained on Trigger's skull, and Jake's heart continued to race inside his chest.

Grace walked with her head bowed, her thick hair obscuring most of her face. When they reached the wagon, she sucked in a deep, shaking breath and took Bullseye's rope from Jake. She stepped inside and coaxed the griffins forward. "Come on. Trigger, step up. Good boy. Now you, Bullseye. Step up. That's it, good. You're just going for a ride, like you always do."

Once they were inside, she started to undo their halters. The man with the gun knocked its barrel against the bars covering the top half of the wagon. "Leave those on. And get out of there."

"Can't I just say goodbye?"

"You have ten seconds."

Tears streaked down her cheeks and melted into the griffins' feathers as she wrapped both arms around their necks. Trigger picked at strands of her hair with his beak while Bullseye let out a series of soft, muted sounds like a chick's chirping.

"I love you both so much," she whispered. "I'm sorry. I'm so, so sorry."

"Time's up. Let's go."

She squeezed between her griffins and exited out the back of the wagon. Jake was there waiting for her. Burke's men climbed onto the front bench and snapped the reins to get the horses moving, and she looked up at him with an entire ocean of grief in her eyes.

He took a step toward her, not knowing what to say or what to do and hating that he'd had any part in her pain. Her hands curled into fists, and for a second, he thought she might hit him, just to get the rage out. Instead, she collapsed into his arms and buried her face in his shoulder. Her tears soaked through his shirt, and quiet sobs shook her body as two pieces of her heart rode away in a cage.

# CHAPTER 20

## SAYING GOODBYE

By late afternoon, the only remnants of Strickland's Circus still on the lot were a couple of vehicles, some straggling troupers, and a few animals waiting for pickup in the otherwise empty ring stock tent. Calico Thunder was among these. Jake stood next to her enclosure and watched her snore. Behind him, Grace sat on the ground in front of the space that had once belonged to Trigger and Bullseye. She'd been there for hours, staring at nothing, saying nothing. Once in a while, new tears streaked down her face as silent sobs shook her body, but she refused all his attempts to comfort her.

They were alone, at least for now. Clarence had grown bored of watching them do nothing after an hour and went to terrorize some of the loiterers into leaving. He came to check on them periodically and deliver a few insults, but Jake was past the point of caring.

He was exhausted, and not just because he hadn't gotten enough sleep the night before. His emotions had been tossed around like a boat on a stormy sea, and the toll it took seemed to weigh him down as much as any physical burden. He just wanted this whole thing to be over already. All of this waiting for the slow but certain end was torture.

Calico Thunder snorted in her sleep, and Jake shook his head. He shouldn't be so eager to rush things along. He was wishing for the end because he was tired of all the waiting, but in doing so, he was also wishing for *her* end. The life of the majestic beast before him was a quickly draining hourglass. Soon, she'd be slaughtered and chopped up into pieces, her hide and blood and bones and teeth sold to create potions that enhanced the forbidden magic people craved.

Morbid visuals of her execution filled his imagination. He tried to shake them off with more comforting rationalizations. Maybe it would be quick. Maybe it would be over before she even knew what was happening. She was old, anyway, and she'd had a good life. Cutting it a little short wouldn't be the worst thing in the world.

He was a terrible person to even think something like that.

But what was he supposed to do? He'd exhausted every option he had, and it still hadn't been enough. Besides, it wasn't like he'd been responsible for any of this. It was Cliff's fault, like so many other things in his life, and why should he take on the guilt of his father's mistakes? This whole mess never should have been dropped on him in the first place.

Something moved behind him, and he turned around to see Grace standing up. She brushed off her skirt and made her way to him. He put an arm around her shoulder, half expecting her to pull away from his touch, but instead, she leaned into him.

She stared at the sleeping dragon. "They're going to take her soon."

"Not just yet," he said, as if that somehow made it any better.

"I keep picturing Trigger and Bullseye locked up somewhere, with some stranger yanking out all their feathers and then beating them when they try to fight back.

What kind of a life is that?" She wrapped her arms around her stomach. "Maybe it would be better if they just killed them, too. Like they're going to do with Calico Thunder."

Her breath hitched as she put her hands over her face and shook her head. "What am I even saying? That's horrible."

He squeezed her shoulder. "It's not. You're just trying to find a way to cope."

"I hate this, Jake. I've never felt so helpless before."

Her words opened a hole in his chest that felt like a physical wound. He wished he knew how to take that feeling away from her. She was the strongest person he knew, and anything *but* helpless.

A cool breeze hit his shoulder blades as someone opened the tent flap behind them. They both turned around, and Otto took off his hat as he nodded to each of them in turn. "Hey boss, Miss Hawkins. A bunch of us are getting ready to leave now. We thought you might want to see us off."

"Already?" Jake asked. There were still a couple more hours left in the afternoon, and Burke had agreed to let them stay until evening.

Otto shrugged. "Clarence is pressuring us to leave, and there's nothing left for us here anyway. Might as well get going while there's still some daylight."

"All right, then." He took Grace's hand, and they followed Otto to the road, where the last of the troupers and a few straggling roustabouts had gathered to bid each other a final farewell. Clarence stood by watching them with his hands in his pockets.

Grace dove right into the group and made her way around to each person, but Jake couldn't bring himself to do the same. He wasn't sure how welcome his goodbyes and well-wishes would be at this point. Judging by the cold looks that sometimes drifted his way, the others still hadn't entirely forgiven him for the way all of this had played out. So instead, he stood on the sidelines and watched while the others embraced and exchanged parting words.

They began to drift away in twos and threes, some heading toward town while others set off up the road to the train yard. Otto gave Jake a smile over his shoulder, then took Thelma and Alice's hands in each of his and headed for the train. They carried everything they owned in the packs on their backs.

Bruno broke off from a group heading into town and made his way over to Jake. The rims of his eyes were red, and his beard and mustache glistened with fallen tears. He cleared his throat as he reached out a hand. "I suppose this is it, then."

"I suppose it is." He moved to shake the dwarf's hand. Instead, Bruno pulled him forward and down to his level, then threw his arms around his shoulders in a tight, slightly awkward hug.

Jake patted his friend on the back before pulling away. "Stay in touch."

"I will. You should come into town with me for drinks when you're done here."

"I ain't really in the mood."

"Oh, come on. It could be fun. One last hurrah before we all go our separate ways." He pulled out a small card and stuck it in Jake's hand. "I'll be at a place called the Cockatrice Club. You'll need this to get in."

Jake glanced at the card. A small, printed image of a fire-breathing rooster adorned the front. He stuck it in his pocket and smiled at his friend. "Take care of yourself, Bruno."

"You, too." He picked up his knapsack, gave Grace one last embrace, and headed down the road into town with a pair of former clowns.

Now, only Jake, Grace, and Clarence remained at the edge of the road. Clarence stretched his arms out to his sides and yawned. "Well, that was touching, but we still have work to do. Come on, Jakey boy. It's time to get that dragon loaded up. We're going to need your help."

Jake glared at the ogre. "Figure it out yourself. I ain't helping you with anything."

Clarence shrugged, unconcerned. "Fine. But there's only one way I know of to get a big beast like that to do what you want. Sean's a little better with the violence than I am, but since he's not here, I guess I will just have to *figure it out myself.* Isn't that right?"

Jake clenched his jaw. He didn't want Calico Thunder's last memories of the circus to be filled with pain and fear—at least not while he could still do something about it. "All right, you've made your point. I'll help you."

Clarence grinned. "Atta boy. Let's go."

Half an hour later, Jake and Grace stood in the back of Calico Thunder's transport truck as the dragon turned herself around to face them. Grace was feeding her pieces of roast chicken the cooks had left behind after lunch, and she snuffed at her hand with a low growl as if to ask where the next morsel was. Grace tossed a leg into the air, and Calico Thunder raised her neck to snap it up before it hit the bars at the top of the cage.

Jake stood on her left side and gave her a few pats on the shoulder. The more he tried not to think about where she was going and what would happen to her next, the more those unpleasant thoughts intruded in his mind.

After a few more seconds, it became unbearable. He was suffocating. He needed to get away from here.

He headed for the door and tugged on Grace's hand as he passed. She pulled away, choosing to stay behind. Jake hopped down onto the dirt. He kept walking and took deep breaths until he could feel air filling his lungs again, but the tightness in his chest remained.

Behind him, Grace murmured a soft goodbye to the noble creature. "I'm going to miss you. You've been such a good girl. You don't deserve any of this."

Clarence's harsh voice interrupted the moment. "I'd appreciate if we could wrap this up quickly."

Jake forced himself to turn back around. Grace cupped Calico Thunder's wide snout in her hands and kissed her right between her nostrils. She wiped a few tears from her eyes as she walked away. Clarence offered his hand to help her off the truck, but she swatted it away and climbed down on her own.

Clarence gave a thumbs-up to the truck's driver, and the engine rumbled to life. Grace grabbed Jake's hand and held it tight. A few more tears made their way down her face as she stood there completely rigid, but she didn't make a sound. Together, they watched the truck pull forward to the road.

Calico Thunder stared out the bars of her cage and let out a muted cry. It sounded almost like a question, and her eyes seemed to pierce right through Jake's soul. Dragons were intelligent beasts—he'd always believed that. Intelligent enough to guess the cruel fate that awaited her? Maybe. Intelligent enough to know he'd done everything in his power to prevent this?

He could only hope.

A mixture of guilt, anger, and misery burned inside him like a hot iron. The heat intensified the farther away Calico Thunder got, until finally he couldn't take it anymore. He hung his head.

In the end, it didn't really matter what his intentions had been. The outcome was the same. The circus was gone, and an amazing, innocent creature was going to die because he hadn't been able to stop the inevitable.

His father's face flashed through his mind, and for a few moments, all he could feel was rage. He wanted to scream and rant and throw things at the man for all the trouble and pain he'd caused. Wherever Cliff was now, Jake hoped he could see this mess for himself, could watch as the legacy he'd sacrificed so much for was demolished thanks to the reckless choices he himself had made. He clamped his jaw shut and clenched his hands tight to keep all the anger from exploding out of him in a roar.

Grace tugged on his hand and shot him a look, and he loosened his too-tight grip on her fingers. The sound of the truck's engine was fading away, and it vanished from sight as it went over a hill and turned a corner.

Clarence took a few steps toward them and pulled out his lighter and a cigar. He started to offer one to Jake, then seemed to think better of it and stuck the case back in his suit jacket. After lighting the cigar and taking a long puff, he broke the silence. "Well, I guess that's it, then. Our business is concluded."

Jake looked around at the empty lot. Only a single car remained, a shiny black coupe that had apparently been left for Clarence to drive. "We're free to go, then?"

"Yes. I'd be happy to give you two a ride into the city if you need it. I know a few good hotels where you could stay."

Even after knowing him for a month, Jake still couldn't tell whether Clarence was as ignorantly insensitive as he seemed or if he simply enjoyed irritating people. He shook his head. "No thanks."

"Are you sure? It might be a little tight in the car, but I'm sure you two lovebirds don't mind sharing a seat."

"We'll walk," Grace said tersely.

"All right, then. I guess this is goodbye." He extended a hand. When Jake didn't return the gesture, he just shrugged and tucked the hand in his pocket. "I know things have always been a bit tense between us, but I appreciate the hospitality your people showed me while I traveled with you."

"Burke didn't give us much choice."

"Maybe not. Still, thank you. And I'm truly sorry about what happened in Griffinsburg. It was just business, you understand. Despite what you think of me, I don't take any pleasure in beating up men who are so much smaller and weaker than me."

Jake resisted the urge to roll his eyes. "Goodbye, Clarence."

He blew cigar smoke out into the air above them and grinned. "Goodbye, Jakey boy."

# CHAPTER 21

## LOOKING GLASS

They walked in silence in the quickly fading daylight, their long shadows stretched out in front of them on the road ahead. Jake carried his most important belongings in a bag slung over his shoulder and a wooden crate that was digging splinters into his palms. Grace carried a bag of her own in addition to her cauldron filled with her entire stockpile of potion ingredients. The rest of their things would be taken east by train to the coastal city where the circus had its winter quarters—the closest thing to a permanent address either of them had.

The buildings that made up the city of Ravington began to close in around them as they continued on. Houses and picket fences lined the streets at the outskirts, and lights began to flicker on in the taller structures up ahead. Soon, they were surrounded by cars and shops and fellow travelers going about their business under the bright city lights.

They'd have to find a hotel room for tonight. Tomorrow, who knew? That was up to Grace. Whatever she decided, Jake would go along with it. It was the very least he could do to give her some sense of control over her circumstances after so much had been taken away from her.

Control. The idea almost made him laugh. For so long, he thought he'd been in control of the situation with Burke. He may not have had any say in how he'd ended up indebted to the mob, but he'd been so certain that he could control the outcome. Every time a new obstacle had come up, he'd dealt with it the best way he knew how. Every time something pushed him back, he'd fought to stay a step ahead. In the end, none of his efforts had made a difference. He'd been playing a losing game the entire time.

So how much control did he really even have over his own life? The most significant parts of it seemed to revolve around a series of unfortunate accidents and decisions made by others. Being abandoned by his father, the rodeo mishap that had ended his career, Cliff's reckless financial decisions, inheriting a traveling circus he'd never asked for and never wanted. All of it well beyond his control, and yet those were the same things that had had some of the biggest impacts on his life.

The old, familiar animosity began to stir inside him—just a little bit—before being snuffed out by his own exhaustion. He was tired of being angry and resentful, tired of carrying around the hurt from things he couldn't change. It took too much energy. He could curse his father and feel sorry for himself forever, or he could pick himself up and do something about the parts of his life that were still under his control.

They rounded a corner onto a busier street, and Grace cleared her throat. She hadn't said a word to him since Calico Thunder had been taken away, but now, she broke the silence. "Hey, Jake?"

"Yeah?"

"I think I owe you an apology."

He blinked. That certainly wasn't what he'd expected. "You don't have to—"

"No, just listen. All those things I said yesterday about you giving up—I'm sorry. I know you did the best you could. And I know you were just trying to protect all of us, including me. I shouldn't have said those things."

"It's all right." Her words had been harsh, but they weren't wrong.

In a way, he *had* given up. The truth was he could have fought harder, could have made different choices. Instead, he'd evaluated the risks before him and decided it was better to lie down and comply with the mob's demands than to put up a fight. Easier to let them take control while he sat back and played the victim when things didn't go his way.

Part of that was because he was afraid. So afraid he'd been willing to compromise what he knew was right by putting his own safety before the lives and well-being of the animals under his care. But part of it was simply because it was familiar. He'd been playing the victim for years, blaming his accident and his father and now Burke and the mob for the misfortunes in his life.

He caught sight of his own reflection in a shop window and frowned. He'd been weak and cowardly—not traits he was proud of. He should have done better. He *wanted* to do better. But this was reality, not some storybook where the heroes saved the day and then rode off into the sunset to live happily ever after.

Except...what if they could do just that? He stopped walking and turned to face his reflection again as the beginnings of an idea began to take shape in his mind.

He shook his head. It was a stupid idea, just exhaustion and threadbare emotions talking. It would never work.

Grace came to rest a few steps ahead of him and turned back. "Jake?"

He swallowed the words on the tip of his tongue. He ought to keep his crazy idea to himself. He'd gotten her involved in enough of his problems already, and in the end, it hadn't done a lick of good.

But the image of Calico Thunder staring at him through the bars of her cage pushed its way to the forefront of his mind.

What did he have left to lose?

Before he got Grace's hopes up, he needed to make sure that what he was planning was even possible. He shifted his crate to one hip and reached into his other pocket for the card Bruno had given him.

"What are you doing?" Grace asked.

He flipped the card over to show her. "Let's go find Bruno."

She sighed and shook her head. "I don't think music and a couple of drinks are going to make me feel any better right now."

"It's not about the drinks." He picked up his crate again and started walking. "Come on. Just trust me."

♦ ♦ ♦

They found the Cockatrice Club without any trouble and were granted entrance after showing their card to the man at the door. The interior was large and crowded, and it took Jake a minute to spot Bruno sitting at the bar. A curvaceous dwarf woman in a short dress had her arms draped over his shoulders and was giggling into his ear.

Jake and Grace set down their belongings in a corner near the door, then wove their way through the crowd to Bruno. He didn't see them until Jake tapped him on the shoulder.

"Jake! Grace!" He stood and threw his arms around them, nearly knocking his beer off the counter in the process. "I didn't think you'd come. Here, sit down."

He snatched a nearby stool from the man who had just vacated it and pulled it up next to him. Jake let Grace take it and stood behind her.

Bruno sat back down. The dwarf woman cleared her throat and asked, "Who are your friends, sugar?"

"Oh, right. Florence, this is Jake Strickland and Grace Hawkins. They were on the show with me."

"Call me Flo." She tilted her head and gave Jake an inquisitive look. "Jake Strickland—as in Strickland's Circus?"

"Yes, ma'am."

Her red lips turned down in a sympathetic pout. "Oh, you poor thing. Bruno was just telling me about how you lost everything. Such a shame. I never had a chance to see your show, but my brother went once and said you were all real entertaining."

"Thank you."

Bruno drained the pint glass in front of him and motioned to the bartender for another. "You want a drink?" he asked Jake and Grace. "It's on me."

Jake shook his head. "That's all right. I just came here to see you. I need a favor."

He raised an eyebrow. "Oh really? And what might that be?"

"Your mirror enchantments—you can use them to find somebody, can't you?"

"I suppose, as long as I could figure out where they were based on their surroundings."

"You didn't tell me you were an Enchanter!" Flo squealed.

Bruno beamed and winked at her. "I was working up to it."

Jake interrupted before his friend could get any more distracted. "What about animals? Could you use the mirror enchantment to talk to an animal, or to find an animal?"

Grace gave him a curious look while Bruno considered the question. He took a long drink from the new glass the bartender had set in front of him before responding. "I've never done it before, so I'm not sure, but I don't see why not. I imagine the biggest challenge would be getting them to even recognize you were trying to communicate. With training, maybe. A dog or an elephant or a dragon might be smart enough to learn, but I don't see why you'd want to teach them a trick like that. Is this for some kind of new act?"

Jake ignored the question. "You could use the enchantment to find them, though? To figure out where they were based on their surroundings."

"Theoretically, yes."

Grace took his hand. "Jake, what's this about?"

"If I told you I might have a plan to rescue Calico Thunder, would you be willing to help me?"

Her eyes widened. "Really?"

"Well, I ain't sure if it'll work yet, but I think we might have a shot."

She gave his hand an excited squeeze. "Of course I'll help. Did you even need to ask?"

"It might be dangerous."

"I don't care. We have to at least try."

Jake turned back to Bruno. "Care test that theory of yours?"

"Sure. But I'll need a mirror."

"Oh! I have one," Flo said. She reached into the beaded purse at her waist and pulled out a compact mirror.

Bruno gave her a quick peck on the cheek as she handed it to him. "Thank you, darling." He opened the mirror and held it up in front of him. "Calico Thunder, you said?"

Jake nodded.

Bruno closed his eyes for a moment, then touched his fingers to the surface of the mirror. When he pulled his hand away, the reflection showed a darkened area surrounded by large buildings, some made of brick and others made of wood. They appeared to be warehouses of some sort. Most looked abandoned. The windows had all been punched out and then boarded up or left open and exposed to the elements.

Jake leaned forward to get a closer look. "I don't see her anywhere."

"Our mirror should be linked to whatever glass surface is closest to her," Bruno said. "By the looks of things, there aren't any other windows or mirrors right where she is."

"Burke probably doesn't want anyone spying on his operations."

"Yes, this seems to be as close as we can get."

"Look!" Grace pointed to something at the edge of the compact. A pair of silhouetted figures walked from the corner of one warehouse to another. One was thin and human-shaped. The other was longer and bulkier, with cat-like rear legs and a hooked beak protruding from its face. "It's a griffin. It has to be Trigger or Bullseye. They must be holding them in the same place."

"Maybe," Bruno said. "I'll try to find one of them instead. Maybe we can get a different angle."

He touched his fingers to the glass again. The reflection didn't change. He tried a second time. The reflection shifted, but it looked much the same as before—the night sky and a bunch of old buildings. A light seeped out from the bottom of a wide door on one of them, but there was no way to see any activity inside.

"What does that mean?" Grace asked.

"It could mean my enchantments aren't working the way I thought they would," Bruno said. "But it's more likely that Calico Thunder and the griffins are indeed being held in the same location. It could be they're keeping all the animals there. We just can't get close enough to see them."

A big, blocky shape sat on the road across from one of the warehouses. "That's our truck," Jake said, pointing. "It's Calico Thunder's transport truck."

Bruno peered closer. "You're right. I'll bet the reflection we saw earlier came from the mirrors on that truck. The angle looks just about right."

"So where are they exactly?" Grace asked.

Bruno shrugged. "Your guess is as good as mine. Maybe inside that building with the light, but maybe not."

Jake continued to search the scene for some kind of identifying feature that would give them a clue about where this was. All he could see was a name on the side of one of the buildings. The paint was chipped and faded, but he could just make out the words—*Grady's Salvage Co.*

That told him basically nothing.

He turned to Flo. "Do you know where this is?"

She shook her head. "Sorry, honey. It doesn't look familiar. I just moved here a couple weeks ago. I'm still learning my way around."

Jake sighed. This was starting to look like a dead end, but he couldn't give up yet. Not after getting Grace's hopes up.

He glanced around the crowded club. "We could ask someone else."

Grace stood up. "Sure. Someone in here must know where that is. I'll start on that side, and you can start over here."

"I don't think that's a good idea," Flo chimed in. She leaned closer and lowered her voice. "I've heard this place does a lot of business with the Viterian mob. Most joints here in Ravington do. You ask the wrong person, or the wrong person hears you're asking questions, and they'll know you're up to something before you even find out where you need to go."

Jake shot Bruno a look. Just how much had he told this woman? There was no sense in being annoyed with him now, though. Flo was right. They needed to figure out where these warehouses were, but they couldn't risk tipping the mob off.

"What about Malone?" Grace said.

Jake shrugged. "What about him?"

"He's from here, isn't he?" She nodded to the compact in Bruno's hands. "He might know where this is. And he owes us."

Bruno frowned. "Wasn't Malone working with Burke the whole time? How do you know he won't just go ratting you out the second he gets a chance?"

It was a fair point, and Jake couldn't guarantee that wasn't exactly what Malone would do. But he was willing to take the gamble. "Burke said Malone felt bad about his part in ruining our show, but he didn't have much choice. If he was given the chance to help us, I think he'd do it. Even if it's just out of guilt."

Bruno still looked doubtful. "Even if it means turning on the mob?"

"I don't know. But I think it's a risk we have to take."

Grace nodded in agreement. “We have to do something, and we may not have much time. They could be moving the animals out of that warehouse tonight for all we know.”

Jake pulled out his billfold and took Malone’s card from one of the slots inside. It was already getting late, and there was a chance the man might not even still be awake. But it was the best shot they had. “Let’s go somewhere quieter.”

Bruno hopped off his barstool and gave Flo’s hand a squeeze. “Save my seat for me, would you, darling?”

“Of course, sugar. Hurry back.”

Jake led the way to the door with Grace and Bruno trailing behind him. “Isn’t she great?” Bruno said as they meandered through the crowd. “I think I might be in love.”

“I think you might be a little drunk,” Grace replied.

He chuckled. “That may be, but the two aren’t mutually exclusive, are they?”

Outside, the din of the crowd and the music faded away, and Jake handed Malone’s card to Bruno. He only glanced at the man’s photo for a moment before opening Flo’s compact mirror and touching its surface once more.

Malone appeared instantly, and he jerked back in surprise at the sudden appearance of Jake’s face in the mirror before him. The toothbrush in his hand clattered to the floor, and for a moment, he just stared while white froth seeped from the corners of his mouth. His eyes were wide with shock and maybe a little fear. Then he frowned, and Jake wondered if he was even going to engage in conversation at all.

After a few more seconds, Malone calmly stepped back up to the mirror and rinsed his mouth in the sink. After dabbing at his face with a dry towel, he leveled his gaze at Jake. It wasn’t an unfriendly gaze, but it certainly wasn’t a welcoming one, either.

After all the lies Malone had told, Jake didn’t really care if he was uncomfortable. In fact, that was probably better. It meant he had a conscience, and that meant Jake would have an easier time convincing him to help them.

At last, Malone touched his fingers to the surface of the mirror. "Good evening, Mr. Strickland. What can I do for you?"

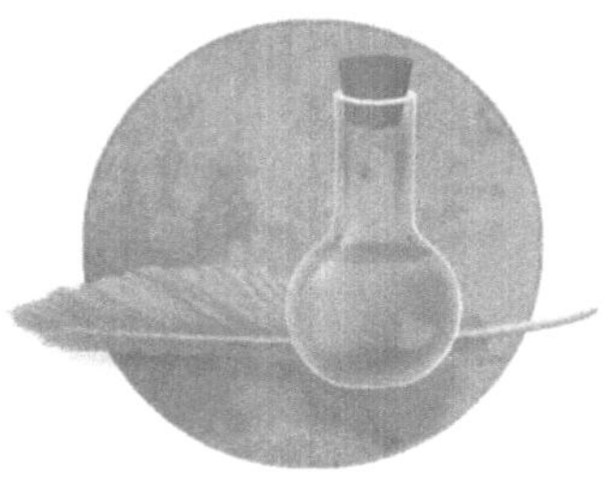

# CHAPTER 22

## MANIPULATIONS AND PREPARATIONS

He should have thought more about the direction he wanted this conversation to take. Now, he didn't know where to begin, so he blurted out the first thing that came to his mind. "You conned me."

Malone's eyes flitted to the side. "Yes, I suppose I did. But you should know I didn't want to."

"I lost everything! People lost their jobs, their livelihoods. You helped them take it all away." The words came out angrier than he'd meant them to, but he *was* angry, and damn it, he had every right to be.

"I'm sorry. You have to understand that if I hadn't helped them, I'd be in your shoes right now. Maybe even worse. I wish I had a better excuse for you, but that's the simple truth of it."

Jake scowled. He hadn't reached out to Malone looking for an explanation, but now, he found he wanted one. More than he wanted a bunch of useless apologies, anyway. "Why did you do it? Why would you work with the mob?"

"Because it was my only choice. He threatened my businesses, my family, my life—everything I care about. After all you've been through this past month, I'm sure you can understand that."

It wasn't the answer he wanted to hear, but it rang true nonetheless. They weren't so different, he and Malone, both driven to do things they never would have considered if not for the desperation the Viterian mob had forced on them. Still, Jake continued to glare at the old man in the mirror.

Malone sighed. "You're angry. I understand that. But Burke's been pulling this same racket on me for two years now. Blackmail, extortion, intimidation—you name it. I've tried everything I could think of to get rid of him. I even went to the feds, but it didn't do a damn bit of good. The mob has more power than they do, and they know it. The only reason Burke finally agreed to get off my back is because I helped him take your circus. I still don't understand what he wants with it, but be grateful you don't have anything left that's of value to him. At least now, he'll leave you alone."

As he spoke, his composure dissolved into a heated fury, and his bony, withered hands were clenched so hard they trembled. Jake's own anger began to simmer down. As much as he hated what Malone had done, he couldn't help pitying him. Jake had only dealt with Burke and the mob for a month, and even that had felt unbearable at times. After two years, it was no wonder Malone had become so desperate.

"He wanted the animals," he said.

Malone tilted his head in confusion. "What?"

"Burke. He wanted the circus because he wanted the animals. The mob's making a killing off this Ban, but the ingredients for the charms and jinxes they've been selling are hard to come by. They can get those ingredients from some of the circus animals."

"Oh, those poor, innocent creatures." Malone pressed his palms together in front of his lips and shook his head. "What a terrible fate."

He had been so delighted by Calico Thunder and the other animals when he'd come to visit the circus, and he sounded genuinely distressed by the news of what had befallen them. Maybe Jake could play on those sympathies. "That's why I'm reaching out to you. We wanna rescue some of the animals. Specifically, we're trying to save our dragon. Burke plans to kill her. We have to get to her before that happens."

Fear returned to Malone's eyes. "Oh. Well, that's certainly a...bold plan. I can't condone any action so sure to evoke the mob's wrath, but it's not really my place to tell you what to do. I wish you the best of luck." He started to reach toward the mirror like he was about to cut off the conversation.

"Wait! We need your help."

He shook his head. "I'm sorry, but I don't think there's anything I can do. Quite frankly, I'd rather not be involved."

"It ain't anything dangerous, I promise. We just need a location."

Malone drew his hand away from the mirror and mulled this over for a few seconds. "I just got rid of them, you understand? I don't want to do anything that draws their attention."

"They'd never know you were involved, I swear. Please, Mr. Malone. If you still have any guilt about what you did to me, my show, the people who worked there, the animals—this is how you make things right. This is how you ease your conscience."

Malone sighed and pinched the bridge of his nose. He stayed that way for a while, not looking at Jake, not looking at anything, just squeezing his eyes together like he could shut out the world and everything that was happening. Finally, he looked up. "All right, then. What is it you're looking for, exactly?"

"We think they're keeping her in some warehouse, maybe here in Ravington, but maybe not. They can't have gone too far, though, so it's gotta be somewhere close by."

"That's all you have?"

Jake tried to recall the details of the scene Bruno had shown them earlier. "The windows have all been shattered and boarded up, and one of the buildings had some big, white lettering—Grady's Salvage Company. You have any idea where that might be?"

Recognition sparked in Malone's eyes. "Yes, I think I do. The warehouse district on the east side of town, right at the edge of the old lake. There was a big fire years ago, after the lake dried up. Most of the buildings were abandoned, but I know Burke's men still use some of them periodically. Last year, feds raided the place, but the mob moved right back in afterward. I think that's when they cleared out all the glass and shattered the windows to make sure no Enchanters could spy on them."

"Is it guarded?" Jake asked. "Do you know how many people are usually there?"

"Not many. Not since Burke started moving his operations out of Ravington. If they're keeping the animals there, it's just temporary. He'd leave a few men with them, and they'll be armed." He shook his head. "I really don't think you should go through with this. Something terrible is bound to happen."

Jake ignored the warning. "Thanks. You've been very helpful."

Bruno closed the compact mirror and stuck it in his pocket. "Are you really going to go through with this?"

Jake looked at Grace, who nodded resolutely. He wove his fingers between hers. "We are."

The worry lines across Bruno's brow deepened. "You heard Malone. The mob has armed men posted at that warehouse. And it's not like you can just sneak in and then sneak back out again with a dragon and two griffins—not without them noticing."

Grace glanced at the door of the speakeasy with a sly grin. "Armed guards won't be a problem. After all, we've got a full arsenal of our own right here."

♦ ♦ ♦

The Caster behind the bar watched with shrewd eyes while Grace counted out the bills from her envelope and laid them on the counter. It was nearly all of her final wages from the circus, but she handed it over without a second's hesitation. "That should cover it."

The Caster flipped through the bills and nodded his approval. After pocketing the money, he pushed a varied pile of bottles and jars over to her. Some held powders while others held liquids and vapors in a range of colors, some dark and opaque while others were light and translucent. Grace stared at them with delight for a few seconds, then began to carefully wrap them up individually with pieces of her own clothing. Jake helped her pack them into her bag.

On her other side, Bruno had his arm around Flo's waist while they watched the bottles and jars disappear from the counter one by one. Flo's eyes were wide, but Bruno had fallen into a state of nonchalance after realizing he couldn't convince his friends to give up their crazy plan.

"Are you sure that's not overkill?" Flo asked.

"Maybe," Grace replied, "but I'd rather be over-prepared than not prepared enough."

"Sure," Bruno said with a yawn. "But running around with that many sleeping jinxes could be hazardous. What if one breaks? What if it knocks you out instead of Burke's guys?"

"That's why we're wrapping them up. We'll be careful."

"And what happens if you put Calico Thunder and Trigger and Bullseye to sleep, too?"

"That's what the wakefulness charms are for."

Jake smiled. She'd thought of everything. It felt good to see her happy and hopeful again. Maybe this was a crazy idea, but having a shared sense of purpose made him feel optimistic in a way he hadn't for a long time.

"What are you going to do once you free them?" Flo asked.

Jake started to open his mouth to answer, then stopped himself. He hadn't thought much past getting the animals free and into the truck. After that, they'd drive... *somewhere.* But he had no specific location in mind and no idea what came after that. How was he going to keep Grace safe after they stole from the Viterian mob?

"We'll head west," Grace said. It slipped out of her mouth like they'd been planning the trip for months. "We'll go to the coast and get on a ship, head overseas, join up with a new circus in some foreign country. They're always looking for new talent, and they'd be foolish turn down a trained dragon like Calico Thunder." Her fingers brushed against Jake's as she picked up another bottle. "It will be a new adventure, just the two of us."

Flo sighed wistfully and laid her head on Bruno's shoulder. "Sounds romantic."

Jake placed the last bottle inside Grace's bag and strapped it shut. "All set?"

Her eyes gleamed with excitement. "Let's go."

She stood up, and Bruno patted her arm. "Good luck, both of you. I'll try not to be offended that you didn't even ask me to come along."

Grace laughed and bent to give him a hug. "You wouldn't have said yes, anyway. Not when you've found such good company here."

Flo blushed. "It was nice to meet you both."

"You too," Jake said. "Bruno, thank you. For everything."

Bruno clasped his hand. "You're welcome. I'm glad you asked. And you be sure to send me an invitation to that wedding of yours once you get settled in somewhere. I'd be honored to be your best man."

Jake grinned. "I can't imagine asking anyone else."

He followed Grace to the exit, where they picked up the rest of their belongings. She swept the door open, and a cool breeze greeted them. Jake paused in the doorway to look back at his friend. Bruno gave him one last wave before returning to his conversation with Flo.

Grace took his hand and gently pulled him outside. "You ready, cowboy?"

He closed the door. "Ready."

# CHAPTER 23

## SILENT PRISON

They got a cab to drop them off at a hotel on the east side of town. From there, it wasn't hard to find the old warehouse district Malone had spoken of. The streets were dark in this part of town, and there was barely enough starlight to see where they were going. The old, abandoned warehouse buildings that rose up before them were merely black shadows against a dark sky. The lack of visibility was frustrating, but it meant they'd be harder to spot by any of Burke's men who might be guarding the place, and that could work to their advantage.

They flattened themselves against the side of a building. "Where do we go?" Grace asked.

"Let's see if we can find the truck," Jake replied. "Or that Grady's Salvage building."

"Okay. Hold on." She rummaged around in her bag for something. There was a snick and a light hissing noise, then a small orange light illuminated the half-used matchbook in Grace's hand. She handed it to Jake. "Here, give me some light."

The match burned out as she crouched down and opened up her bag, and Jake struck a new one. He watched her dig around, feeling the wrapped bottles and jars, quickly uncovering some of them and moving on to the next when she didn't find what she needed.

He burned through another match. "What are you looking for?"

"These—I think. Light?"

He brought the tiny flame closer, and Grace held up four glass containers. The two larger jars contained a thick, blue substance. Some kind of charm, but Jake couldn't remember what it was for. The other two smaller vials held a familiar reddish-orange liquid. Luck charms.

The match he was holding burned out. "What are the blue ones?"

"Stealth charms. Good for sneaking around. Here, take them."

He stuck the matchbook in his pocket and took one of each type of charm, then uncorked the larger bottle. "Bottoms up."

The stealth charm hit his tongue in a gelatinous goop that burned like hot peppers. He forced himself to swallow, then chased it down with the more pleasant-tasting luck charm. Once finished, he set the empty containers on the ground next to Grace's.

"Let's hope that worked," she said. "Come on."

He followed her along the edge of the building. When they reached the corner, she leaned out to peer into the darkness ahead before they continued on. So far, they hadn't seen or heard any signs of activity anywhere, but that only meant they hadn't yet gotten to where they needed to be.

Jake's heart pounded a steady, too-fast rhythm against his chest, and the hair on his neck stood on end. Even with the stealth charm, he heard every footstep, and the jars in Grace's bag occasionally clacked together in a way that seemed to echo through the empty spaces between the deserted buildings. Each time, he whipped around to look behind them, half expecting one of Burke's men to jump out with a machine gun. No one ever did.

They saw no signs of life until they made their way much deeper into the maze of buildings. A faint glow appeared up ahead, and Grace turned to Jake with a finger to her lips. As they continued on, the light slowly grew, offering them a little more visibility. They reached the end of the wall they'd been walking alongside and stopped to reassess their surroundings.

Jake spotted something out of the corner of his eye and tapped Grace on the shoulder. It was Calico Thunder's transport truck, and her face lit up when he pointed to it. He peered around the corner to check for any further signs of activity. The light was coming from somewhere beyond the truck—possibly the same building they'd seen with the mirror enchantment earlier—but he couldn't see from this angle.

Cautiously, he stepped out from the cover of the building and started to head for the truck. He held up a palm to Grace, indicating that she should wait behind. Out here, he felt exposed and vulnerable, but he entrusted his safety to the stealth charm he'd just taken and his own hyper-aroused senses on alert for anything dangerous around him.

The truck grew closer with each step. When he reached it, he crouched low behind its frame and shuffled forward until he was positioned directly behind the rear tire. He looked out toward the dim light he and Grace had been following.

Farther ahead, a wood-framed warehouse stood with its door propped open. Light spilled out onto the grimy street outside, and a few shadows flitted across the ground. Standing perpendicular to the building was a taller brick structure. In the light, Jake could just make out the faded letters of Grady's Salvage Co. painted across the top. They were in the right place.

He motioned for Grace to come forward, then turned his attention back to the lit warehouse. If Burke had any men posted here, this was where they should be.

Almost as if on cue, a lone figure outside passed in front of the open door, silhouetted against the light. Jake tracked the man's movement, noting the shape of what appeared to be a pistol in his right hand. He kept walking until he disappeared from Jake's line of sight behind another building.

Grace reached the truck and crouched down beside him. She peered past him to the light up ahead. "You think they're in there?"

He nodded. "I just saw someone go by, maybe some kind of patrol. The others are probably inside."

"What do you want to do?"

"Let's just watch for a few minutes."

They did, huddled together in silence behind the truck's tire. The same man with the gun passed by three more times at fairly regular intervals. Sometimes, he stopped and looked into the darkness ahead—toward the circus truck, toward them. Apparently, he couldn't see them from here, but if they were going to make a move, they needed to time it right, and they needed to act before anything changed.

"The next time he goes by," Jake said, "let's get our things in the truck and unlock the back, just in case we need to get out of here in a hurry. After that, we can head up the road to that brick building there and plan our next move."

"We'll have to find some way to take out that guard," Grace replied.

"Maybe it's time for one of them sleeping jinxes."

"Maybe, but we don't want it to wear out too fast."

"Let's just move up ahead first. We should have a better view inside the warehouse from there. Here he comes." He pulled his head back behind the truck tire and waited until it was all clear.

Grace, facing forward, was able to peek over the top of the truck bed and through the bars of the cage. "He's looking this way again. Go on, there's nothing to see here. That's right. And...he's gone."

They shuffled over to the cab of the truck, deposited their belongings inside, and shut the door. Jake went to the rear and dialed the combinations to unlock the three heavy padlocks that kept the door closed. They'd have to wait to open it so as not to alter the truck's profile in a way that might alert the guard, but doing this part would save them time later.

"He's coming back," Grace hissed.

Jake dropped down behind the tire again. "Did he see me?"

"I don't think so. No, there he goes. Come on."

She stood and set off at a brisk pace down the road, cradling her bag of charms and jinxes in both arms to keep the jars from jostling against each other. Jake set off after her. They reached their destination and flattened themselves against the brick wall just as the man patrolling the warehouse came around the corner again.

From here, they could hear the faint crunch of his footsteps on the gravel. Jake waited until the sound grew faint again before he risked sticking his head out to get a look at their new surroundings.

Through the half-open door, he was able to peer into the warehouse. Cages lined the wall from floor to ceiling as far as he could see. Some were larger than others, and nearly all of them held living creatures. He recognized a few of his own—a pair of phoenixes, some wyverns, and the fairy box from the menagerie—but there were many more not from Strickland's Circus.

A flash of orange, brown, and white scales caught his eye, and he spotted the spiked end of Calico Thunder's tail inside a larger cage just behind the door. It lashed back and forth like an angry cat's, a sure sign of her irritation.

It was only then that the quiet hit him. Many of the caged animals struggled in their enclosures and opened their mouths to vocalize their frustration, but there was no sound. At least, no sound that Jake could hear. The entire warehouse must have been cloaked with some kind of enchanted sound barrier.

Aside from the cages and the animals, he could also see a group of men sitting in the center of the warehouse on wooden crates. They were playing cards. One of them had put four crates together to accommodate his larger frame, and Jake's gaze flickered up past the man's suit and tie to his face. Clarence. He laid his cards out for the other men to see, and a familiar fanged smile pulled at his lips.

Grace shook his shoulder. "Jake, the guard."

He pulled back. The sound of the guard's approaching footsteps sent a chill up his spine in the dead silence of what should have been a tumult of panicked shrieks, growls, and roars. He clenched his jaw and waited until the guard moved on before turning to Grace.

"They have more than just our animals in there."

"Did you see Calico Thunder? What about Trigger and Bullseye?"

"I saw her, but not the griffins. They've gotta be in there, though."

Grace stepped past him to look into the warehouse herself. She raised a hand to her mouth and drew back. "There are so many of them. We have to get them out of there."

"We will. Did you see Clarence?"

Her eyes widened. "He's *here*?"

"Him and about four other men, plus the one walking around outside."

"We have plenty of sleeping jinxes—enough to knock them all out for a good hour or so."

"Even Clarence?" The ogre's larger frame and unique physiology could alter the effectiveness and duration of the jinx.

"Maybe. We'll work fast. It will be fine."

Even if it wasn't, they weren't turning back now. After what he'd seen inside that warehouse, any lingering doubts Jake might have had about the risks involved in this undertaking had disappeared.

"It'll be better if we hit them all at the same time," he said. "You think you can take the one outside on your own?"

"Absolutely." She was already digging through her bag for the jars they needed.

The guard came by again as she divvied out the jinxes. She grouped four on the ground for Jake and kept two for herself. These jars were larger than all the others and contained a swirling purple vapor that shimmered when it caught the light. All they had to do was break the jars near their targets, and the escaping mist would put them into a deep sleep.

For good measure, they each took one of the shirts Grace had used to wrap the jars and tied it around their noses and mouths. The jinxes wouldn't be of any use if they somehow managed to knock themselves out in the process of executing their plan.

Jake scooped three of his jars up in one arm and pressed them against his chest. He gripped the fourth in his free hand, ready to throw once he had a good shot. He nodded to Grace. She nodded back, and they darted out of cover to head for the warehouse.

They got closer and split off, Grace following the path of the patrolling guard while Jake approached the warehouse from an angle that would shield him from view of its occupants. He got right up next to the door, but even from there, he couldn't hear any of the animals.

He inched forward until he could see where he was aiming and lobbed one of his jars inside. It shattered when it hit the ground, but there was no sound of breaking glass. The men jumped up, sending cards flying into the air. A purple haze was already rising from the ground, but the jinx would need at least a few seconds to take effect.

The sharp sound of breaking glass came from somewhere to his right. The men inside the warehouse reached for their guns, but not before Jake threw his second and third sleeping jinxes. His eyes met Clarence's as the purple mist thickened. The ogre raised his weapon. Jake threw his final jar and ducked back behind the door.

More glass shattered, and a gunshot rang out. Jake flinched, half expecting Clarence's bullet to hit him. He breathed a sigh of relief when no pain followed the sound.

The sound. If he was hearing the gunshot, then it couldn't have come from inside the sound-eliminating barrier of the enchanted warehouse.

That shot had been for Grace.

# CHAPTER 24

## FREE

Jake scrabbled to his feet and took off running toward the sound of the gunshot. He didn't look back, even though he couldn't yet be sure his sleeping jinxes had actually taken effect, even though Clarence could still be coming after him.

It didn't matter. All he cared about was getting to Grace.

He leaped over something sprawled across his path. A body—the guard.

But even if the guard was down, that didn't mean she was okay. She could still be hurt.

He kept running. "Grace!"

She emerged from the other corner of the building. "What?"

He gripped her by the shoulders and looked her up and down. "Are you hurt?"

"I'm fine." She placed her hands over his. "It's okay. Calm down."

"The gunshot—I didn't know if—"

"Well, it was a pretty close call." She grabbed the side of her skirt and put her finger through two identical ragged holes in its fabric. "It's a good thing we had those luck charms, huh?"

He eyed the blackened edges of the holes. *Bullet* holes, in her clothing. Too close for comfort. He pulled her into an embrace and held her tight to reassure himself that she was really okay. “I don’t think I’d count getting shot at as being lucky.” He kissed her forehead, ignoring the loose strands of hair that tickled his nose.

“Maybe not, but it could have been worse.” She pulled back and took his hand. “Come on. Let’s go do what we came here to do.”

They stepped over shards of broken glass and made their way back to the warehouse door. It had been flung wide open, and Clarence lay on his stomach with one half of his body inside and the other outside. He still clutched his gun, which looked pitifully small in his meaty hands. Jake pried the weapon free and stepped over his awkwardly splayed limbs with Grace trailing behind him.

Inside, the enchanted silence barrier that made sound inaudible to outsiders lost its effect on them. The few animals that hadn’t succumbed to sleep tried to make sense of what was happening, emitting low growls and dazed whimpers from the cages all around. These cages extended far beyond what Jake had been able to see from outside. They lined every wall end to end and were stacked from floor to ceiling in most places, like the entire warehouse had been transformed into some kind of animal prison.

Jake found Calico Thunder in a cage too small to even turn around in. She raised her head when he approached and purred a low growl. He stuck his hand through the bars and rubbed her snout. “We’re gonna get you out of here, old girl. Just hang on a minute.”

Grace made her way over to the other side of the warehouse, stepping over crates and peacefully dozing mobsters in her path. Narrow stalls lined this side of the building, each one tightly packed with as many as five or six animals.

She headed for the section of stalls that held griffins. Jake followed. Most of the creatures were asleep, but even without calling their names, it wasn't hard to pick out Trigger and Bullseye amongst the others. They were easily the cleanest animals in the group. The others were covered with dirt, grime, and what looked like fecal matter. Considering the complete lack of cleanliness in the stalls and the fetid stench seeping through Jake's makeshift face mask, that wasn't surprising.

Grace surveyed the animals and shook her head. "This is even worse than I imagined. Look at them—some of them are sick. I think that one might be dead."

He looked to where she pointed. A scrawny body with matted fur lay motionless in one corner, eyes closed and beak open. If it was still breathing, Jake couldn't see the rise and fall of its chest from where he stood.

"We can't leave them in here like this," she said.

"Well we can't take them all with us. We could call the police, but I have a feeling that's not gonna make much difference."

"Not if what Malone said about the feds is true."

"So what do you wanna do?"

She shrugged. "If we wake them up, we could just...set them all free."

"Maybe. But we've got no way of knowing if they're even fit to survive out there on their own. Some might be as tame as Trigger and Bullseye—raised by humans, never had to hunt their own food. Captivity is all they know."

"This isn't captivity. This is cruelty." She looked up at him with determined eyes. "Maybe they won't all survive out there, but some will. That's better than dying in here, or dying weeks or months from now when they've been sold and stripped and tormented. If that's the best we can do for them, we should give them that chance."

She made a valid argument, and freeing the animals would throw a wrench in the mob's operations, at least for a little while. That was something Jake could take pleasure in. "All right. But we should hurry."

"We should be able to keep the wakefulness charm contained in here, but we'll need to move Burke's guys first."

Jake turned around to look at the bodies sprawled out on the warehouse floor. Hauling the humans outside would be a challenge, but not impossible. Moving Clarence, however, was another story. He probably weighed as much as the two of them put together. Twice.

Grace dug around inside her bag again. It was far less full and bulky than it had been when they left the Cockatrice Club. She pulled out two identical vials of an opaque, green liquid.

"What's that?"

"Strength charm," she replied brightly.

He shook his head and smiled. "You really did think of everything, didn't you?"

She shrugged. "I wasn't sure if we were going to have to fight our way in."

"You don't think I could hold my own in a fight?"

She rolled her eyes in mock annoyance. "I'm sorry. Do you remember what happened the last time you got into a three-on-one fight against Burke's goons?"

"I lost that fight on purpose."

"Is that so? I'll take it you don't need this, then." She dangled the strength charm in front of him.

He snatched it away from her and pulled out the cork. "I don't see any reason why I should make life harder on myself."

She shoved him playfully in the arm and uncorked her own charm. "Cheers."

Jake braced himself for whatever unpleasant taste was about to follow, but surprisingly, the strength charm didn't taste like anything. He could barely feel it on his tongue at all. "That's it? Are you sure this thing is even working?"

"Let's go find out."

She made her way over to the nearest mobster and bent to pick him up by the arms. Jake took his legs. Together, they lifted the man with surprising ease and carried him to the door. It took a little careful maneuvering to get past Clarence, who was still blocking most of the doorway, but they managed.

"Not bad," Grace said as they laid the man down next to the guard outside. "But these don't last very long. Let's get Clarence next."

Moving the ogre took considerably more effort, and they were both panting by the time they got him outside. But thanks to the strength charm, it wasn't an impossible task. He murmured a little in his sleep, so Grace opened up their last sleeping jinx and held it directly in front of his face for a few seconds to make sure he was fully knocked out.

They carried the rest out one by one. Calico Thunder watched them with drooping eyes, occasionally opening her jaws in a yawn as she fought off the lingering effects of the sleeping jinx. Jake could feel the strength charm wearing off by the time they moved the last man, and he and Grace ended up half-dragging him outside to lie with the others.

"I'll start waking the animals up if you want to go get the truck started," she suggested.

"Sure. I'll be back in a minute." He headed out into the dark at a jog. When he reached the truck, he removed the padlocks from the back of the cage and pushed the door wide open. After cranking the engine to a rumbling start, he left it idling and returned to the warehouse.

Inside, four empty jars sat open on the floor, one for each side of the building. Jake recognized them from the speakeasy; they'd previously held the yellow-tinted vapor of the wakefulness charm. Now that it was dispersed into the air, most of the animals were starting to wake. Their shrieks and growls filled Jake's ears as he made his way to Grace, who was engaged in a happy reunion with Trigger and Bullseye in their stall. Trigger nuzzled her face and pulled at pieces of her hair with his beak, and Bullseye stood on his rear legs with his talons hanging over the wood door. It looked like he'd been trying to climb out to reach Grace but had gotten stuck halfway.

She giggled and pushed Bullseye's face away from hers. "Okay, boys. That's enough of that. How about we get you out of here, huh? Would you like that?"

She grabbed two lead ropes from a hook on the door and handed one to Jake. They each looped one over a griffin's neck. A spark lit Grace's eyes, and she reached for the latch holding the stall closed. "Here we go."

She opened the door. At first, none of the griffins moved. Jake tugged on Bullseye's lead rope. Once he had walked out of the stall, the rest followed. They were hesitant at first, as if they were unsure what to make of being allowed to simply walk out the door. They moved forward in a tight huddle, but when Jake pulled Bullseye away from the pack, they began to spread out.

Grace opened the second stall full of griffins and gently shooed them out to join the others. Moving slowly across the warehouse floor, they stretched their wings and looked around. A few became curious, sniffing at crates and peering into the cages of the other animals. A young griffin meandered over to the open door, then let out a high-pitched shriek to call for his mother.

The others turned toward the sound, and the juvenile stepped outside. His mother followed. Soon, the rest were sprinting for the door as fast as their legs could carry them. They spread their wings as they burst out into the night and leapt into the sky with varying degrees of finesse. A few came crashing back down, but they managed to get airborne on their second or third attempts.

Before long, all of them were gone except for Trigger and Bullseye. Jake watched their black shadows grow smaller against the starlight and silently wished for them to find health and safety in their new freedom.

He led Bullseye over to Grace. "Truck's ready to go. You wanna load them up while I finish in here?"

She took Bulleye's lead rope. "Sure. I'll come help you with Calico Thunder when I'm done."

She led Trigger and Bullseye outside, and Jake turned back to the stalls and cages. He freed the unicorns next. They thundered past him in a flurry of pounding hooves and ran straight out the door without any cue. The giant spiders took a little more prodding, and Jake stood up on one of the stall dividers to swat at them with his hat. He suppressed a shudder as he watched them skitter out the door on their numerous spindly legs.

Using a set of keys he'd taken off one of the mobsters, he unlocked the rest of the cages one by one. Each key had a label that matched its lock, so it didn't take long to find and open them all. Soon, all kinds of creatures were running, hopping, flying, and slithering around the warehouse. Jake shooed them to the door as best as he could manage.

Grace nearly tripped over a pair of pygmy hippogriffs on her way back in. She laughed at Jake's efforts to pry a particularly ill-tempered wyvern off the bars of its cage. "You've been busy, I see."

"Yeah. I'm sure the people of Ravington are going to love us for this."

"Most of the animals were headed the opposite direction, away from the city." She reached into the cage to hold onto the wyvern's legs before it could grasp at the bars again. "Besides, the people of Ravington allowed this to happen right here in their own city, so I'm not feeling too much sympathy for them at the moment."

"Maybe they didn't know."

"And maybe they will now." She glanced over her shoulder at the rest of the warehouse and shook her head. "I wish I'd known it was like this. I don't think I'll ever buy another charm or jinx again."

Jake finally managed to unhook the wyvern's last claw. Flapping wings buffeted his face, but he and Grace managed to carry it to the door to set it free. It flew off, and he straightened his hat on his head. "Almost done."

Calico Thunder growled in her cage, and Grace laughed. "Someone's getting impatient."

"Your turn's coming," Jake said to the dragon. "Just hold on."

Grace followed him to the opposite corner of the room. "We should hurry. The farther we are away from here when Clarence and the others wake up, the better."

"It's just these left, then we can take Calico Thunder and go." He tapped his fingers against the top of a long, glass tank, and a few of the luminescent fairies inside flew up to see what the noise was about.

"These are ours, aren't they?" Grace asked.

Jake rubbed his thumb along the metal plate at the top of the tank, engraved with his father's name. "They were."

He unlatched the tank lid and lifted it up. The fairies that had been hovering near the top flitted out. After a few seconds, the rest joined them, darting through the air and casting little spots of color around the warehouse. They soon found their way to the open door, and for a few brief moments, dozens of multicolored lights flickered like fireworks against the darkness. Then they scattered and disappeared into the night.

Jake and Grace returned to Calico Thunder's cage. He unlocked the door and swung it wide open. "Come on, old girl. Let's get moving."

The dragon stretched her forelegs out in front of her, then stood. It took some precision to back herself through the narrow door. Her wings were still bound against her body, and one of the bottom points got wedged between two of the cage bars. She growled in pain and took a step forward before trying again, this time shifting her weight to the other side so she could squeeze through.

"That's it, good girl," Grace cooed. She reached into the bag still slung over her chest and pulled out the last jar. The liquid inside was a pale, milky yellow—the mild dragon intoxicant Calico Thunder loved so much. Jake held his breath before he could catch a whiff of the rancid substance, and Grace unscrewed the lid. "Look what I've got for you. Let's go to the truck. Come on."

She followed them outside. They retreated from the warehouse, and Jake glanced over his shoulder to the side of the building where they'd left the sleeping mobsters. They all still appeared to be slumbering on, completely oblivious to the events of the last half hour.

He smiled to himself. They were actually going to pull this off.

They continued down the street at a steady pace. Once they reached the truck, Jake hurried to open the door. Trigger and Bullseye were already huddled together comfortably on the far end, right up against the cab.

Grace reached between the bars of the cage to set her jar down. She slid it back, and some of its contents sloshed out onto the floor. Calico Thunder started to stick her head through the door, then stopped.

"Step up," Grace said.

She stood frozen right where she was, nostrils flaring as she sniffed the cool air.

Jake ran his hand along her left foreleg. "Come on. Step up."

She still didn't budge.

"Do you think it's the griffins?" he asked.

Grace shook her head. "She's had to ride with them a few times before, and we've never had any trouble."

He moved up a little so he was directly within her line of sight and stroked her neck. "Come on, old girl. What's the matter? There's nothing to worry about in there." He smacked his palm against the bed of the truck. "Step up."

Calico Thunder sniffed inside, snorted, and raised her left foreleg. The truck shifted under her weight as she placed it on the floor.

Grace patted her on the side. “There, that’s the way. Good girl.”

Before she could get another leg in, a harsh voice called out behind them. “Stop! What do you think you’re doing?”

# CHAPTER 25

## LAST RIDE

Jake whipped around to see Clarence barreling toward them at a dead sprint. In the same instant, Calico Thunder backed away from the truck and pivoted to face the oncoming threat, nearly knocking Grace to the ground with her tail. Trigger and Bullseye thrashed inside the cage. A second later, they shot out the open door, wings unfurled, and took to the sky.

Calico Thunder stretched her neck out toward Clarence and roared, every muscle in her body tense. Jake clamped his hands over his ears to block out the deafening sound, but Clarence didn't seem the least bit intimidated. He kept coming.

Grace darted in front of the dragon and said something to try to get her attention, but her snarls drowned out all other sound. They were never going to get her in the truck now, and even if they could, it wouldn't matter. Trigger and Bullseye were already gone.

A new idea came to him—a wild, desperate, risky idea he wasn't even sure would work. But given the alternative of being apprehended by Clarence and turned over to the mob for punishment, it was their only option.

Before he could talk himself out of it, he put one foot on Calico Thunder's rear leg and hoisted himself up onto her back.

She stopped roaring and turned her head to look at him as he straddled her spine. The sharp points on every single tooth in her bone-crushing jaws glistened in the moonlight, and Jake immediately second-guessed his decision. She'd never bitten anyone before, but there was a first time for everything. There was a reason all the dragons he'd ever ridden in the rodeo had been muzzled.

Grace stared up him from the ground with wide eyes. "What are you doing?"

"Come up here."

"Get down from there!" Clarence yelled.

Calico Thunder whipped her head back around and roared at the ogre again. He was closing in fast.

Grace hurried to the dragon's forelegs, and Jake reached down to help her climb up. She sat behind him and wrapped her arms tight around his waist.

Clarence tried to find some way past the dragon's snapping jaws, but even in her old age, she was quick. Each time he got too close, she stretched out her neck to bare her teeth or swiped at him with her claws. It was all Jake and Grace could do to keep themselves from being thrown to the ground. Jake's hat flew off his head, but he didn't bother checking to see where it landed.

A familiar spasm of pain shot up his spine at the dragon's lashing movements, but he just whooped and clung tighter to her mottled scales. For years, he'd dreamed of riding a dragon again. He'd longed for the thrill and the glory and the reckless abandon of it all. Just one last time, even if it hurt like hell.

Calico Thunder strained against the ropes binding her wings, trying to employ her natural defensive instincts. Dragons often spread their wings to appear larger than they really were when threatened, but she couldn't even do that now.

He called out to Grace. "Give me your knife."

She wrapped one arm tighter around his waist and reached into her pocket with the other. When she handed him the knife, he flicked it open and began sawing at the thick ropes binding

Calico Thunder's wings. At one point, she thrashed so violently he nicked the thin membrane stretched between her bones and drew blood, but she didn't even seem to notice.

Clarence kept bellowing at them from the ground. "You stupid, ugly beast. Let me through! Jake! If you don't get down, there'll be hell to pay."

The more he shouted, the more riled Calico Thunder became. Jake nearly tumbled from his precarious perch. It was only because of Grace's solid grasp on him and the familiar, practiced grip of his knees on the dragon's back that they managed to stay on.

He still had a few fibers left to saw through when the rope snapped. It whipped through the air, and Calico Thunder's wings burst open like two sails caught in a gust of wind. Jake dropped the knife as he went sliding off her back.

His boot hit something hard on the way down—her bent foreleg—and he used it to propel himself back up. Grace helped him scrabble into position behind Calico Thunder's wings and shoulders.

"What now?" she asked. She had to yell to be heard above Clarence's shouts and the dragon's snarls.

Jake wasn't sure. Calico Thunder hadn't flown in years. He didn't even know if she could anymore, and there was nothing to stop her from simply shaking them off her back once she got tired of them, either now or once they were airborne. But they couldn't stay here.

"Come on, old girl." He reached forward to massage the joint where her left wing connected to her shoulder. "You're free. Get us out of here."

The gesture seemed to trigger something. Instead of fanning her wings out at their assailant, she raised them up on either side.

Clarence took advantage of her momentary lapse in attention to dart past her head and forelegs. He reached up, grabbed hold of Jake's boot, and started to pull. "No one steals from the Viterian mob! No one."

Jake found a handhold in the scales and clung to it with his fingertips. Grace attempted to kick at Clarence's hand, but she couldn't reach far enough—not without sliding off the dragon's back herself. With every movement, Jake's grip slipped a little more.

Just when he was sure he was going to fall, a flurry of feathers and fur plummeted from the sky. Shrieking, Trigger and Bullseye clawed at Clarence's arms and face. He cried out in fury and pain. The distraction lasted just long enough for Jake to break free of his grasp. Clarence stumbled back, clutching his face as blood dripped down from his chin.

Trigger and Bullseye flew up into the air again, and Calico Thunder started running. Jake used the rhythm of her huge, powerful steps to push himself back into place, then leaned forward until he was nearly lying flat between her shoulder blades. Clarence snarled curses and threats as he sprinted after them.

Calico Thunder pumped her wings. She lifted off the ground for a few yards, then faltered and hit the ground hard. She skidded to avoid running into a building, but her right hip smashed up against it anyway. The impact rattled Jake's jaw.

Grace reached to her side and gave her a pat. "You can do it. Keep trying!"

The dragon snorted in response and took off running again. She lifted off, wavering for just a moment before she got into a good rhythm. A brick building loomed just yards ahead, and she veered up sharply to avoid hitting it. She climbed higher and higher, far beyond what would have been the enchanted barrier of any rodeo arena Jake had ever ridden in. His stomach dropped, and every inch of his skin prickled with goosebumps.

Clarence, the truck, and the warehouses grew smaller and smaller beneath them, and the stars somehow seemed to glow bigger and brighter up here. Grace's arms were wrapped so tight around him he could barely breathe, and her fingers dug into his chest as they continued to ascend. She screamed, and he couldn't tell if it was from sheer terror, uninhibited joy, or both.

He let out a cry of his own. His fingernails bled where he'd clung to the dragon's scales, and his back ached like it had been repeatedly struck by lightning, but this was worth it. He couldn't remember the last time he'd felt so free and alive.

Calico Thunder leveled off and began to soar through the night sky at a smooth, even pace. A few seconds later, Trigger and Bullseye came up on her left to fly beside her. They squawked a greeting, and she snorted in response.

Jake sat up a little straighter and looked over his shoulder at Grace. "You okay?"

She nodded, loosened her arms from around his waist, and nestled her chin against his shoulder. The air whipped strands of her hair into Jake's face, and she laughed as she combed through it with her fingers to flow out behind her. "I get it now," she said.

"Get what?"

"I mean, I used to think you were crazy. What kind of person voluntarily climbs onto the back of an animal that could easily kill them, just for the sake of entertainment?"

He grinned. "Yeah, maybe it is a little crazy."

"It is. But I think I get it now, and I'm sorry you lost it. It must have been amazing."

"It was." He looked up at the stars like an endless, glittering ocean above them and put one hand over hers. "But this is so much better."

♦ ♦ ♦

They flew west, away from Ravington, away from the mob. They didn't land until just before dawn, when they spotted a train bridge that crossed over a river in the wilderness below. The stars had faded away, and daylight was just beginning to light the world once more.

They circled the riverbank, and Grace commanded Trigger and Bullseye to descend. Calico Thunder followed. When she landed, Jake and Grace slid off her back and stumbled into the grass, their muscles taut and sore from the night's flight. The animals bowed their heads to the water and took a long drink.

Jake reached out to pat Calico Thunder's leg. "You did good, old girl. Real good."

She raised her head, water dripping from her jaws, and stared at him with her one good eye. She blinked once, then went back to drinking.

"What now?" Grace asked, scratching Bullseye under the chin.

"The mob's gonna be out for our blood after this," Jake responded. "We oughta steer clear of their territory for a while. I liked your plan. Head west, get on a ship, find some other show to join up with overseas. That is, if you're still willing to drag me along."

"Isn't that what you signed up for when you asked me to marry you?"

"Only if that's what you agreed to when you said yes."

"Looks like we're stuck with each other, then."

He smiled. "I think I saw a town a couple miles back. The tracks should cut right through it. We could get on board there and keep heading west." He motioned to the animals. "I just don't know how we're gonna get these guys into town with us."

"They'll follow us. Or they won't. Maybe they'll fly off on their own to live in the wild." She patted Trigger's shoulder. "And that's okay. There are worse things that could happen to them."

Calico Thunder finished drinking. She yawned and stretched her forelegs out in front of her, then laid down at the edge of the river and closed her eyes.

Jake laughed. "I don't think we need to worry about them taking off just yet. Looks like she's ready for a nap."

"I can't say I blame her. She's had a long night."

He nodded and laid down in the grass a few yards away from the dragon with his hands behind his head. The new position helped to ease some of the throbbing in his back.

Grace put her hands on her hips and stared down at him. "After everything we just went through, you really want to sit here and be lazy?"

"It ain't my fault. Blame the dragon."

"Don't you think we should keep moving?"

"Sure, but I don't think we're going anywhere until she's good and ready."

Trigger and Bullseye turned circles in the grass a few times, then laid down together with their heads tucked under their wings. Grace threw her hands up in dismay. "Oh, and you too, huh? Traitors."

"You might as well give up," Jake said. "Come on down here and get some rest."

"Fine, but only for a few minutes."

"Sure. We'll just let the dragon and the griffins know they have to stay on *our* schedule, then."

She shook her head and laid down next to him. "You're no help at all, you know that?"

He chuckled and stared up at the clouds overhead. A feeling of peace settled over him with the warmth of the rising sun. Calico Thunder, Trigger, Bullseye, Grace—they were all free. And so was he. Or at least as free as a man could be with the Viterian mob's bounty on his head.

But what was life without at least a little danger? He could go anywhere he wanted, do anything, but the only place he wanted to be was with Grace. He would follow her anywhere, on any adventure she was willing to bring him along.

He kissed her forehead and wrapped an arm around her shoulder to draw her closer. "Just a few minutes. Then we'll go wherever you wanna go."

# GLOSSARY

ADVANCE MAN – A circus employee who travels ahead of the show to put up posters publicizing the circus' arrival

ANNOUNCER – The person who announces the acts to the audience during a circus performance

BAGGAGE STOCK – Animals used for hauling and transporting (as opposed to *ring stock*)

BIG TOP – The main tent of a circus used for performances

CASTER – A magic user who can cast charms and jinxes, either directly onto a person or through the use of specially crafted potions

CHARM – A form of magic that enhances a certain characteristic or ability of a person; charms may be cast directly but are more commonly infused into special potions that activate once a person consumes them.

CLEM – A fight

COOKHOUSE – The place where circus personnel eat

ENCHANTER – A magic user who has the ability to enchant inanimate objects, thereby giving them special properties

ENCHANTMENT – A form of magic that gives a special property or effect to the targeted inanimate object

FIRST OF MAY – A worker or performer in his/her first season. Shows usually played the season's opening spot on May first, so the term refers to someone who is new to circus life

GLAMOUR – A specific type of illusion that changes the appearance of the wearer

GREASE JOINT – The grill or concessions trailer

HEALER – A magic user who has the ability to heal illness and injury, often supplemented through the use of potions

HEY RUBE! – The traditional battle cry of circus people in fights with townies

HIPPODROME TRACK – The oval area between the rings and the stands/audience

ILLUSION – A form of magic that creates a distortion of senses; illusions may affect any or all of the five senses

ILLUSIONIST – A magic user who can create illusions

JINX – A form of magic that dampens a certain characteristic or ability of a person, or otherwise produces a negative effect; jinxes may be cast directly but are more commonly infused in special potions that activate once a person consumes them.

THE MARCH – The street parade, often from the train yard to the performance location

MENAGERIE – A collection of captive animals on display for the public

PATCHES – Circus workmen whose job is to smooth things over with the townies (usually when they wanted their money back) so they wouldn't cause problems

RING – The circle in which circus acts are presented. Strickland's Circus is a three-ring circus, with a large center ring and two smaller rings on either side.

RING STOCK – Circus animals that perform in the show

ROUSTABOUT – A circus workman or laborer

ROUTE – The show's annual itinerary, a schedule of towns to be played

ROUTE BOOK – A journal containing notes about each stand, such as location, conditions, attendance, anything noteworthy about the performance, etc.

SIDEWALL – The canvas wall that hangs below a canvas top. A circus tent is made up of the canvas top with its sidewalls attached.

SLEDGE GANG – A crew of workers who pound in tent stakes

SPECTACLE (SPEC) – A colorful pageant or grand entry which is usually the opening number of a show. All circus performers and animals are presented in full regalia along with the band.

STAND – Any town where the circus plays, as in *one-night stand*

TOWNIES – Townspeople; any outsiders

TROUPER – A circus performer; anyone who has spent at least one full season with the show and is accustomed to the life and demands of the circus

WINTER QUARTERS – The location where a show stays during its off season

## Dear Reader

Thank you so much for reading this book. I hope you enjoyed it. Now that you're finished, please consider taking the time to leave an honest review. Reviews are especially important to indie authors and can help others make informed decisions about their reading experience, which allows the book to reach its target audience.

Follow me social media to stay up to date on my writing, and please feel free to reach out. Your questions and comments about the story and characters are always welcome and appreciated.

tahernandez.com
tahernandez@tahernandez.com
Twitter: @ta_hernandez5
Instagram: @ta_hernandez5
facebook.com/tahernandez05

Acknowledgements

This book has gone through so many variations to become what it is now, and I never would have been able to stick with it for so long if it weren't for all the amazing people who encouraged me along the way.

I am so grateful and deeply indebted to the wonderful group of beta readers and critique partners who helped me transform an aimless, underwhelming, and underdeveloped short story into a book that will forever hold a piece of my heart. Taylor, Alex, Kimberly, Fran, Kate, Janine, Elissa, Kathy, and Rachel—you guys are superstars and I so appreciate your incredibly helpful feedback and encouraging words regarding this story.

Thank you to my family for encouraging not only my writing endeavors but all the other dreams I've wanted to pursue. I especially want to thank my husband and forever best friend, Alex, who has always been there to cheer me on and provide whatever kind of support I've needed along the way.

And finally but perhaps most importantly, thank *you*, reader, for investing your time in this story. The fact that I get to share my words with others means everything to me, and I'm forever grateful to readers like you who are willing to step into the world of my imagination for just a little while.

## About the Author

T. A. Hernandez is a science fiction and fantasy author and longtime fan of speculative fiction. She grew up with her nose habitually stuck in a book and her mind constantly wandering to make-believe worlds full of magic and adventure. She began writing shortly after reading J. R. R. Tolkien's *The Lord of the Rings* many years ago and is now happily engaged in an exciting and lifelong quest to tell captivating stories.

She is a clinical social worker and the proud mother of two girls. She also enjoys drawing, reading, graphic design, playing video games, riding her motorcycle, and making happy memories with her family and friends.

♦ ♦ ♦

## Other Works by T. A. Hernandez

**The *Curse of Shavhalla* series**
*Tethered Spirits*

**The *Secrets of PEACE* series**
*Secrets of PEACE*
*Renegades of PEACE*
*Survivors of PEACE*
La Sangre Tira Mucho: A *Secrets of PEACE* short story

**Short Stories**
The Eligibility Formula
Reparations

www.ingramcontent.com/pod-product-compliance
Lightning Source LLC
Chambersburg PA
CBHW030530310726
48979CB00010B/1865/J
* 9 7 8 1 7 3 4 0 3 3 0 0 7 *